SHENANDOAH AUTUMN

COURAGE UNDER FIRE

by
Mauriel Phillips Joslyn

Illustrated by
Martha Frances Huston

WM KIDS
6

WHITE MANE KIDS

This White Mane Books publication
was printed by
Beidel Printing House, Inc.
63 West Burd Street
Shippensburg, PA 17257-0152 USA

In respect for the scholarship contained herein, the acid-free paper used in this book meets the guidelines for permanence and durability of the Committee on Production Guidelines for Book Longevity of the Council on Library Resources.

For a complete list of available publications
please write
White Mane Books
Division of White Mane Publishing Company, Inc.
P.O. Box 152
Shippensburg, PA 17257-0152 USA

Library of Congress Cataloging-in-Publication Data

Joslyn, Mauriel, 1955-
    Shenandoah autumn : courage under fire / by Mauriel Phillips Joslyn.
        p.   cm.
    Summary: Living in the Shenandoah Valley of Virginia during the time of the Civil War, fifteen-year-old Mattie proves to be a woman of courage even as conflicts rage around her.
    ISBN 1-57249-137-x (alk. paper)
    1. Shenandoah River Valley (Va. and W. Va.)--History--Civil War, 1861-1865--Juvenile fiction. [1. Shenandoah River Valley (Va. and W. Va.)--History--Civil War, 1861-1865--Fiction. 2. United States--History--Civil War, 1861-1865--Fiction. 3. Virginia--Fiction. 4. Courage--Fiction.]   I. Title.
PZ7.J7894Sh   1998
[Fic]--dc21   98-21429
                                                                    CIP
                                                                    AC

PRINTED IN THE UNITED STATES OF AMERICA

DEDICATION

For all the boys who wore the gray
and the girls who loved them.

CONTENTS

Prologue... vii
Chapter One.. 1
Chapter Two... 5
Chapter Three 13
Chapter Four 20
Chapter Five 26
Chapter Six 29
Chapter Seven 32
Chapter Eight 35
Chapter Nine 40
Chapter Ten 46
Chapter Eleven 56
Chapter Twelve 60
Chapter Thirteen 63
Chapter Fourteen 67
Chapter Fifteen 74
Chapter Sixteen 79

Chapter Seventeen 84

Chapter Eighteen 88

Chapter Nineteen 94

Chapter Twenty 98

Chapter Twenty-one 104

Chapter Twenty-two 111

Chapter Twenty-three 114

Chapter Twenty-four 117

Chapter Twenty-five 122

Chapter Twenty-six 126

Chapter Twenty-seven 130

Chapter Twenty-eight 136

Chapter Twenty-nine 142

Epilogue 147

Author's Note 149

PROLOGUE

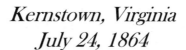

Kernstown, Virginia
July 24, 1864

"Bienville Blues!" called Captain DeCourcey. "Fix bayonets!" His horse fought the bridle with anticipation, as the captain watched his company prepare to attack. "Cha-a-arge!"

His mount bounded forward, and the unleashed line of Louisianians briskly stepped from a quick to a double-quick run.

Will Hamilton's blood was up, and he released the tension with a Rebel yell, mingling his voice with those of his comrades. The charging mass of men moved through the stubble of a wheat field towards the Union forces, while their own artillery boomed encouragement in the rear. They had the Yanks on the run, and the instincts of hunters pushed them forward.

Ahead, perhaps 100 yards away, Will could see the blue line briefly rally to fire a volley. An exploding shell hit nearby and the smoke and dust shrouded the field, obscuring the scene. He could only hear the concentrated rattle of muskets ahead, as he temporarily slowed, disoriented by the billowing white smoke. Loading his musket, he looked to his side, searching for Pierre and Jean to maintain a straight line, but he could not make out the shape of any human forms. Then a gentle breeze began to clear the smoke, and he saw gray uniforms slightly ahead of him. He brought his musket up under his arm to the prime position and started to run toward his company, eager to be among the first to hit the faltering Yankee line.

Then something hit him so powerfully, that he was knocked to the ground, propelled into a floating darkness, and the only sensation his mind could identify was pain. It happened so quickly he could hardly comprehend that he had been shot before he lost consciousness, and the sound and fury around him faded away.

The sound of a horse snorting was enough to rouse him from unconsciousness. He flexed his fingers, stiff with dried blood, and remembered what had happened. On either side of him lay boys he knew, now dead. Gathering his wits, he knew he must be careful. Was the horse with friend or foe?

The weakness from loss of blood made his movements slow as he turned his body to peep around the trunk of the oak tree he lay under. There, about fifty yards away, were two horsemen, and relief flooded over him. They wore the gray of Virginia cavalrymen. One man knelt beside the body of a soldier from Louisiana, who was obviously dead. The other man remained mounted, the horses skittish and snorting with fear at the smell of blood.

I have to get their attention, he thought. Breathing as deeply as he could, he called out.

"Help! Help me!" His voice sounded so feeble. What he had meant as a shout sounded little more than a whisper, but the men had heard. They looked around to find the sound, then glanced at each other, listening.

Pulling himself along by grabbing grass and underbrush with his hands, and dragging his legs, he began to crawl toward the open field. If they leave me, I'll bleed to death, he thought. This was his only chance. He threw his last ounce of strength into his voice.

"Help! I'm here. Over here!" He waved an arm, and tried to crawl faster.

The two men looked his way. They had seen him, and started toward him, picking their way over the bodies of his dead comrades, the horses cocking their heads and twisting their ears as they stepped gingerly around the sprawled and still figures on the ground.

"My God! There's one still alive!" As they reached him, the dismounted man took his canteen from the saddle. But before the offered water could be accepted, everything passed into darkness.

CHAPTER ONE

Newtown, Virginia
July 25, 1864

The chirping of crickets and whirring cicadas cut through the thick summer heat. For once the air was relieved of the far-off sound of guns. Matilda closed her eyes and concentrated on the pleasure of bird and insect noises. She let her needlework slip from her hands, and leaned against her chair. The deep front porch kept the air cool and protected her from the hot sun. In a neighboring field a horse neighed to its pasture mate. It was a perfect summer day.

"I hope they've stopped forever," Mattie murmured to herself. The small farming community of Newtown, Virginia had been caught in the crossfire of two warring armies for over three years. Everyone was confident at first that it wouldn't last long, or that they would be spared. But soon they realized that peace was only that lull found between battles. After two years, complacency set in and now no one even mentioned a time when the war would be over. They simply lived by their wits from day to day, thanking

1

heaven if the livestock had been spared or that they had enough food for the next meal.

"Wake up Matilda!" The lilting tones of her mother's Irish accent brought her back to the present. "We've a letter from your father, and it's good news. He will be home on nine-day furlough!" Moira MacDonald could not contain her happiness. Her husband Andrew had been away for six months as a sergeant with the Confederate army. "A friend of your father's in the 33rd Virginia brought the letter just now." "When will he be here?" asked Mattie. After a quick thought she added reluctantly, "Is he wounded?" The words were hard to say.

"No," said her mother with relief, hand over her heart. "Praise God, he is well." Mattie sighed her relief also. So many men had been wounded. And so many had died. Not only men from the Lower Valley but many others from all over the South who had passed through on the army's way up and down the Valley. Mattie thought of once when she had seen the retreating army pass by their home, for the main Valley Turnpike was scarcely 100 yards from their door. She saw men tramping along, slowly and painfully with heads in stained bandages, or arms in slings. Some who had been wounded seriously in surrounding battles had been taken in by families in the area when they were too severely hurt to ride or walk. Mrs. Adams who lived on the neighboring farm had nursed four of them back to health. Her husband was too old to be a soldier and their two sons were away in the army. Three of her charges had rejoined their regiments but one was still recovering at the Adamses' home.

"I'll be going over to see Mrs. Adams now. Jenna has made two pies that I want to take. And I've finished the shirt for the Captain so I'll take it too. Would you like to come along?" her mother asked.

"Yes, I would." Matilda jumped at the opportunity. She got up and followed her mother into the house. "I like Captain DeCourcey, don't you mother? Captain James DeCourcey was the wounded officer Mrs. Adams still had living there, a Louisianian who had been severely wounded in the shoulder. "He's quite handsome, and I especially like his French accent, don't you?"

"Yes, Matilda, he is very handsome, rather exotic don't you think?" said Moira. Mattie nodded.

Although he was much older, closer to her father's age, he had a way of making her feel like a friend. He was quick to confide in Mattie and made her visits quite a treat. Even so, she knew he was grateful to the Adamses, realizing they had saved his life.

Mrs. MacDonald had spent her spare time sewing for the wounded, or helping any way she could in the nearby hospital which had been established at a boarding house in town. But whenever Mattie insisted on coming along, it was usually abruptly denied. "That is no place for a girl of fifteen to be, in the company of men just brought off of a battlefield," her mother would proclaim. When it was a visit to a private home, that was different.

"Wait, Mother, I have something that I made for the Captain that I would like to take too." Mattie gathered her sewing from her lap, and quickly dashed into her room, throwing pins and thread in her basket as she went. She opened a little bureau drawer where she kept small articles she had sewn—handkerchiefs, laces, collars, and samplers. Here too, she had placed a little crocheted cross with a long tassel. She had made it for the Captain to be used as a bookmark, and inspected it to make sure every stitch was perfect. Then, she carefully wrapped it in a piece of plain stationery. Tucking it into her reticule around her waist, she tidied her blonde hair, adjusting the long strands in her hairnet while looking in the mirror, and smoothed her skirts. When she was satisfied with her appearance, she took her straw hat from the dresser, and went to find her mother.

CHAPTER TWO

Captain James DeCourcey stood in front of the washstand, and carefully shaved the last of the lather from his chin. The steam from the washbasin added to the heat of the day. He rinsed the razor off and dried his hands and face on a linen towel, brushing his mustache with his fingers. Standing shirtless, in his uniform trousers, he contemplated his circumstances. He looked in the mirror and studied the ragged red wound of his left shoulder. The bullet hole had healed, leaving a sunken scar, but it was still sore when he moved. It had also fractured his collarbone, making recovery a slow process. But he had been at the Adams's farm for over two months now. How thankful he was to these kind people who had taken him in, a stranger exiled from his home, giving him the care and attention that had saved his life. He wished he could somehow repay them, but here was a long way from a home under enemy occupation, having no way to acquire money or the simple necessities. He relied solely on the generosity of Virginians who knew it was men like himself who were fighting for their state.

A gentle knock came at the door.

"Captain DeCourcey, Mrs. MacDonald and Miss Matilda are here."

"Merci, Mrs. Adams. I will be ready momentarily. Oh, Mrs. Adams," he added as he walked to the door and opened it before she left. "I am afraid I must trouble you to apply my bandage."

"Of course, Captain, I will be right back."

Leaving the door ajar, he went to the armoire and took out a shirt. Putting his right arm through and draping the shirt over his left shoulder, he forgot his sorrows for the moment. He enjoyed the visits of Moira and Matilda. The young girl reminded him of his own two daughters, and they were always pleasant memories. After he began to recover, they occasionally took walks around the farm. He had told her about his wife and daughters, and she had served as a confidánte for his sentimental feelings of homesickness. He would miss her, and especially wanted to leave her something to remember him by. All he had was a miniature flag of Louisiana that his girls had made for him. He had carried it into battle, sewn in the sweatband of his hat for safekeeping. Now that he would be leaving to go back to his company in a few days, this may be the last chance he would have to see Mattie. It was a difficult decision, but he realized he may not live to carry the little flag home. At least if he gave it to Mattie, she would keep it safe. That was much more comforting than the thought that it may be overlooked if he were killed, or worse, defiled by enemy hands who cared not what it meant to him. He made up his mind— to give it to Mattie. He was certain his daughters would agree.

He tucked it into his vest pocket, just as he heard Mrs. Adams and Moira coming down the hall. Mrs. Adams pushed the door open carefully, and seeing that he was dressed, entered carrying some clean linen bandages.

"How does it look today, Captain?" she asked. Moira followed her into the room. He sat in a chair beside the washstand.

"Much better, Mrs. Adams. A little stiff, but I will simply have to remember not to swing from any limbs for awhile," he smiled.

Carefully she bandaged his shoulder lightly, mostly for support and protection.

"I do wish you didn't have to leave so soon. I would like for you to be a little more healed. Just you be careful." Mrs. Adams had grown fond of the polite and gracious company of Captain DeCourcey.

"If I do not get back to my company soon, I'm afraid they will forget who I am and find themselves a new captain," he joked. "Besides, the sooner this war is won, the sooner I can go home. We need all men at the front now." This was added with all seriousness.

The two women exchanged glances. Moira knew how anxious he was to hear from his family. With the Yankee occupation of Louisiana there had been many stories of atrocities, and very few letters from home had gotten through the lines. Under normal circumstances he would have been furloughed with his wound, but going home was impossible, so he concentrated on his army service. Mrs. Adams broke the uneasy silence.

"Well, with your leaving, Ben and I have decided to go to Strasburg to stay with our daughter-in-law and her little ones for a while. With the armies out of Newtown now, the farm should be safe for a few weeks, and Tom will be here."

"We will come and see to things for you. Andrew will be coming home, and he can come by and check on things for Tom while you're gone," offered Moira.

"That would ease my mind," added Mrs. Adams. "I believe that will be good enough for now Captain," she added as she neatly finished tying the bandage.

"Merci, Madame. I do hope Mattie accompanied you?" He turned to Moira.

"Oh, of course. She is waiting downstairs in the parlor. I told her it would probably be good-bye."

Captain DeCourcey stood and finished putting on his shirt. He tried not to wince as he raised his arm, not wanting Mrs. Adams to see how much it still hurt. "I must not keep a friend waiting," he said. "I will join you ladies shortly."

The two women left, and Captain DeCourcey put on his vest, carefully checking the pocket holding the little flag. Then he followed the two ladies downstairs.

Mattie sat in the parlor of the comfortable old farmhouse. The air was cool, and the muslin coverings on the furniture for the season added the illusion that it was not sweltering outside. Her mother had told her that Captain James, as he was affectionately known to her, was returning to his regiment, the 8th Louisiana Tigers. She would miss these visits. He had become sort of a substitute father these past months while her own was away. She would never be able to think of him again without concern for his safety.

As she heard the creak of footsteps on the stairs, and the women's voices, she reminded herself not to be melancholy. Mattie, despite her young age, had learned like all women of the war-torn South that their outward pleasantness and confidence had a direct effect on the men's state of mind. *Perhaps it is my courage that will sustain him in battle*, she thought, when lives hung in the balance.

"Bonjour, Miss Matilda," the Captain bowed graciously, taking her hand. "Hello, Captain," she smiled in return. "Jenna baked two pies, and we've brought them for you. I suppose you can take them when you leave." Mattie tried not to sound sad.

"I also have something for you, Captain," said Moira. She took the folded shirt from some wrapping paper and handed it to him. He unfolded it, studying the neat stitches proudly. It was the only extra shirt he had now. The bullet had destroyed the other.

"I am most grateful, Mrs. MacDonald," he said with a bow. "Now I don't have to worry so much about my appearance. You know, laundry is not priority with soldiers."

"I can imagine," Moira smiled. "I fear to think what kinds of clothes Andrew will be wearing when he comes home. I've made him two new shirts also." The obvious pleasure of the news of her husband's return made her creamy complexion radiant. Mattie was anxious to present her gift, but she preferred to do that alone. The best way would be to go out for a walk, but she didn't feel it proper that she suggest it. Fortunately, she didn't have to. Captain James refolded his new shirt and laid it aside.

"I feel like taking a walk before the heat becomes too intense. Matilda, would you give me the pleasure of your company?" He offered his arm.

"May I, Mother?" asked Mattie, her heart racing.

"Yes, Mattie, only don't tire the Captain too much," her mother warned. "I've brought some sewing for Mrs. Adams to help me with anyway."

Captain DeCourcey escorted Mattie into the hall. He took his slouch hat from the hall tree, and opened the front door. They stepped out on the porch into the late morning sun.

"You have my thanks for rescuing me from drawing room women's talk," he laughed. Then they both laughed as they relaxed their manners and started off down the farm path toward the garden.

"Would you like to see the new foal?" he asked. "It's in the barn."

"That would be Nelly's foal, right?" asked Mattie. "I used to ride her sometimes, before we sold her to Mr. Adams. The Yankees took their carriage horse," she added with distaste.

"I know. Mrs. Adams still gets fire in her eyes when she thinks of it," laughed Captain James.

They walked down toward the barnyard, and went into the cool dark barn. The aroma of fresh cut hay stored above, and warm animal smells in summer heat greeted them. Mattie always liked the smell of the barn, the scent of horses. They heard the quiet contented sounds of the mare chewing her hay. Mattie walked ahead of the Captain to the stall where Nelly stood.

"Hello, girl," said Mattie. "Is that your baby?"

The mare looked at Mattie, and pricked her ears in recognition. She walked over and stretched her neck over the wooden half door of the stall. Mattie patted her affectionately. She looked behind Nelly at the grey, long-legged foal with what looked like a bottle brush for a tail.

"He's a fine baby, Nelly. What shall we call him?"

"I believe Mrs. Adams has christened him 'Colonel Mosby,'" said Captain DeCourcey.

"Then hello, Colonel Mosby." It seemed such a big name to live up to for so small and inexperienced a creature as a foal, she pondered. Colonel John S. Mosby was the hero of the hour in the Valley. His exploits with his Rangers had been legendary for almost two years here, and he had saved Newtown more than once from Yankee cavalry, stealing their supplies and making them shake in their boots with fear of the consequences if he captured any of them.

Mattie turned from the horse stall and faced Captain James, preparing to present him with her gift.

"I have something for you, Captain," she began, taking it from her reticule. It was still wrapped in the piece of stationery. He looked at her, pleased that she was giving him something to remember her kindness by. He took it and unwrapped the little cross with the tassel.

"It's a bookmark. I thought perhaps you would like it for your Bible," she explained.

"I will use it Mattie, and I will always think of you," he said, touched that everyone genuinely seemed glad to have made his acquaintance. He put it in his vest pocket, taking out at the same time the little folded flag.

"And I have something for you, Matilda," he said as he held it thoughtfully before extending his hand toward her. She looked at him, puzzled. *What could he possibly have to give? It must be very precious to him*, she thought as she accepted the gift. Unfolding it, she recognized the pelican emblem of the flag of his beloved state.

"Captain James," she said in awe, and giving him a look of disbelief, not understanding why he would give it to her.

"My daughters made it, and gave it to me the day I left home," he seemed to choke on unseen tears. His handsome face was pale, the soft grey eyes sad and reflective. "I want you to have it Mattie. I don't want to risk losing it if anything should happen—" he left the sentence unfinished, their unspoken thoughts filling in the rest.

"I'm honored to have it, and I will keep it for you until the war is over." She looked at the stitches made by the girls so near her own age.

"I feel like I know them from all our conversations," she said. Carefully, she folded it and put it in her reticule.

"Shall we continue our walk?" said Captain DeCourcey, steering away from the awkward sadness of the conversation. "Yes, I would like to walk down to the pond and see the ducks." "Very well, to the pond—" and he stepped aside as she led the way.

CHAPTER THREE

Mattie and her mother had just driven into the front yard when their house servant ran up to the carriage. Jenna had been with the MacDonalds since they came to the Valley, and was only a few years older than Moira. She was quick and efficient with any task, but now she seemed so excited they knew something had happened.

"Miz Moira," she called as she hurried toward the carriage. Moira halted the horse and glanced toward Jenna. Beyond her, beside the front porch stood three horses, cavalry saddles identifying them as Confederate. Two men in gray uniforms were on the steps, and a third stood with his arm around a soldier leaning on the porch rail. The man seemed limp and Moira guessed he must either be wounded or very ill.

"What's wrong, Jenna?" she asked cautiously. The men looked up in her direction, a little uncomfortably, feeling awkward at being on her porch without invitation.

"These gentlemens is got a wounded sojer wid them. They's needing to talk wid you." Jenna nervously wiped her hands on her apron. She had been interrupted in the kitchen.

"He's just a boy, Miz Moira, just a boy. And he's hurt real bad."

"I will speak with the men. Matilda, you go with Jenna." Moira descended from the carriage and walked over to the men. They tipped their hats. The man holding the wounded soldier nodded in respect. The sergeant spoke.

"Good day ma'am. We're sorry to disturb you and your family, but we need some help. This young man was wounded badly, and needs someplace to stay. He was found this morning, been lying on the field for twenty-four hours. He's lost a lot of blood."

"What about the hospital in town," asked Moira.

"We went there, and they didn't have a spare bed, nor floor space either. But if we could leave him here the doctor will come around and take a look at him."

Moira hesitated. The men fidgeted.

"After Kernstown, the towns are full of sick and wounded. The boy may already be beyond help ma'am," spoke the sergeant with a note of pleading in his voice.

Moira didn't exactly know what to say. But on glancing at the wounded cavalryman she saw a dark and wet stain spreading across his uniform jacket, which had soaked his side and stained his trousers down to the knee. She didn't have the heart to send them away. Instinctively she knew this young man may die. She thought of Mattie, wondering if she should be exposed to that dark side of life. Mrs. Adams would be going to Strasburg and would not be able to tend another wounded man. Besides, she had done it for months now. Moira felt it was someone else's turn.

"Bring him upstairs," she said as she walked past them and led the way.

Mattie and Jenna had gone round to the back porch. Mattie was determined to see what was going on. Her mother always felt she was too young to be subjected to unpleasantness, but she was aware of what happened to men in battle. The war had taught her that. Besides, curiosity was stronger than shock.

"I'm going inside Jenna," she said as she opened the door.

"Yore mama told you to stay wid me," said Jenna in a warning tone.

"I know," said Mattie, too distracted to argue. She didn't care. She tiptoed in the back door which opened into the hall in a direct line with the front door. She saw the sergeant and one of the other men carrying the wounded man upstairs gently, as if he would break. Her mother followed. Mattie walked to the bottom of the stairs and waited, listening to the noises of preparation—her mother's hurried instructions to place him in the guest room, her fussing over linens, and sending one of the men downstairs with the basin pitcher for water. Mattie stepped aside.

"Would you please get us some hot water, ma'am?" he asked, holding out the pitcher. Mattie took it and went back to Jenna, while the soldier hurried back up the stairs.

"Jenna, do we have some water heated?" she asked hurriedly at the back door.

"Yes, Miz Mattie. You wait and I"ll brang it." She took the pitcher and went into the kitchen, joined to the main house by a breezeway. Mattie stood at the door, looking into the hall. The three cavalrymen came down and went out the front door. She heard them as they mounted their horses and rode away. Jenna returned with the water.

"Here it is, Miz Mattie. You gon' take it up?" Mattie thought a moment.

"Yes, I will Jenna. Thank you," she said as she took the pitcher and went back into the hall. As she mounted the stairs, she wondered what awaited at the top. She had seen the stained clothes on the man's right side, and knew he was badly hurt.

She cautiously approached the door of the guest room, opened to a crack, and peeked in. She could see her mother standing by the washstand, with a pair of scissors. The bed was out of sight, and all Mattie could discern was her mother bending, working over something on the bed. Mattie gathered her courage and opened the door. There on the bed lay the wounded soldier. His jacket had been removed and her mother was cutting his shirt off. Moira looked up, startled that it was Mattie instead of Jenna. She recovered her composure, the task at hand too serious to be concerned with Mattie. Maybe it was time for Mattie to see what women had to deal with. After all she would be having her own babies in a few years, and would have to tend sickness and accidents. These were the things expected of a woman with a family.

"There's a lot of blood, Mattie. Does that bother you?"

"No." Mattie lied, not really knowing.

"Then come here and pour some water in the basin. I need your help."

Mattie cautiously went to the washstand, her eyes avoiding the bed. Her mother put the bloody remnants of the shirt in a pile on newspapers on the floor.

"Wet these rags and hand them back," said her mother as she handed Mattie some clean strips of old bed sheets. "He's a terrible mess. The blood has dried and clotted. To be honest I don't know if he will live or not."

Mattie glanced at the man's bloody side. At first she couldn't keep her eyes on the wound, averting them, until after several attempts she could watch. It amazed her that her mother wasn't sickened by it. Instead, Moira worked quickly and efficiently, rinsing the cloths and gently wiping around the gaping hole.

"Keep changing the water," she told her daughter. Mattie poured the red-stained water in a bucket next to the bed, and clean water into the washbasin. Moira looked at her. "Are you alright?" she asked as she swiftly worked.

"Yes," Mattie said, surprised at her own calmness. The wound got less and less bloody, and finally emerged under her mother's gentle but thorough cleaning, a ragged red tear. "The doctor should be here any time. I wanted to have him as clean as possible."

Moira laid a clean cloth across the wound and began to wash his face, hands, and arms. He was dirty and sweaty, his hair matted with mud. Once cleaned and the mud removed, they were surprised to find a boy's face, no more than eighteen or nineteen years old. He remained unconscious the whole time, as lifeless and unresponsive as a doll. Suddenly fear gripped Mattie, as the awful thought struck her.

"He is alive, isn't he, Mother?" She felt repulsed at the thought of touching a dead person.

"Of course he's alive," her mother snickered at Mattie's naivety. "But he has lost a lot of blood, and seems very pale. There seems to be no fever though, and that's a good sign," she felt his forehead as she spoke.

Mattie watched his face. It was a nice face, dark hair and high cheekbones. Wet curls of hair clung to his forehead and at his temples. He had no beard or mustache like Captain James, but Mattie thought how handsome he must be when he smiled. She could not help but question if he would ever smile again.

So far he hadn't moved, hardly seemed to be breathing.

"That will be the doctor," her mother's voice interrupted her thoughts. Mattie had been so preoccupied that she hadn't heard Dr. Johnson coming up the stairs.

Dr. Elbert Johnson opened the door and approached the scene before him. He had viewed this picture many times in the last three years. In his fifties, he was too old to serve as a surgeon for the army, but he volunteered his services at the civilian and military hospitals. That was where he was most needed after all and he had organized the local hospital with the help of the ladies in Newtown for soldiers wounded in the many battles fought between Winchester and Strasburg.

"Good day, ladies. It seems you have things under control. I know your experience, Mrs. MacDonald, so I don't have to tell you what needs to be done."

"Is there anything I can get you, Dr. Johnson?" asked Moira.

"I would appreciate something to drink," added Dr. Johnson. It had been a busy day.

"We have some cider if that will do," replied Moira.

"That sounds good to me," said Dr. Johnson. All the while he talked, he examined the patient, probing the wound, and it made Mattie wince to watch. But the soldier was still deep in unconsciousness. Dr. Johnson listened to heartbeats weak from lack of food and loss of blood.

Moira and Mattie left.

"We'll give him a little while to rest while the doctor tends him," said Moira as they walked down the stairs.

"Can we keep him here, Mother?" asked Mattie, surprised at how she blurted it out. "I mean, does he have to be sent to the hospital?"

"I doubt if he should be moved again, at least anytime soon," said Moira. "I see no reason why we can't look after him. But Mattie," she cautioned, "he is very weak. Be prepared if . . ."

She didn't have to finish the sentence.

"I know Mother," replied Mattie. "But at least we know that we did everything possible to save him." Mother and daughter exchanged knowing looks, and Moira realized that perhaps her daughter was more grown up than she thought.

Later, Mattie went back upstairs to her room. The door of the guest room stood slightly ajar, and all was hushed within. She took the little pelican flag that Captain DeCourcey had given her, and looked at it. "Oh, please let him be safe," she whispered in prayer. Opening her bureau drawer, she placed it with her needlework and other treasures. Then tiptoeing back by the open door, she went downstairs where her mother and Dr. Johnson sat talking.

CHAPTER FOUR

"His name is Will Hamilton, and he's not in the cavalry," said Dr. Johnson. "I found a letter in his pocket, along with a knife and $20.00 in Confederate notes. The letter is his own, presumably he was planning to mail it soon." Doctor Johnson drank his cider leisurely, sitting on the porch with Moira and Mattie. He had been invited to stay for supper and, being a widower, was grateful for the suggestion. The young man upstairs had not regained consciousness, but the doctor was more optimistic than he had been on first examination.

"So far, miraculously, there's no sign of infection. The bullet made a clean entry and exit, not damaging anything internally but causing a bad tear. If we can just keep him alive and let him build up some blood supply, he probably will live."

Mattie was surprised at how much relief she felt at those words. She wanted to know this stranger, who he was, what had happened to him and where he was from.

"He is pretty low, however, and will need to be watched closely. I suggest someone sitting in there with him around the clock for a few days, until he regains consciousness. He will have to be spoon fed awake or not, and given water. The wound should be cleaned, repacked and rebandaged daily to keep out gangrene. Another worry is pneumonia."

He knew that was to be feared as much as a bullet. Many men had been well on the way to recovery when pneumonia set in and death claimed them.

"We have had some success with patients in the hospital avoiding it if they are propped up in bed with pillows. I think that is what we will do with Private Hamilton." After supper, Moira and Dr. Johnson went upstairs to check on their young charge. Mattie followed hesitantly. They went into the small guest room at the top of the stairs. The young soldier had not moved since Mattie saw him earlier.

"I have an old nightshirt of Andrew's here," whispered Moira as she opened the doors of the big armoire in the corner.

"That's fine. I've taken off his trousers and if you would be so kind as to find a couple of extra pillows, we'll get him more comfortable."

Mattie watched her mother and Dr. Johnson as they dressed the limp figure and arranged the pillows so that he was propped up. Although he was very pale, he looked better now that he was free of dirt and blood. The bandage around his waist had a tiny stain where the blood had seeped through.

"I don't want to bend that wounded side too much. But that should be good enough for now. I'll come round in a day or two, if I don't hear from you before, and see how he is. Until then I'll say good evening." He picked up his bag of instruments and started for the door.

"Thank you, Doctor," said Mrs. MacDonald as she escorted him down the stairs. Mattie was left behind.

They didn't seem to notice that she had even been there. Now she stood all alone, looking at this man who was totally dependent on their care. Not sure what to do, she decided not to leave. She pulled up a chair and sat beside the washstand, which was adjacent to the side of the bed, and studied his face once again, more at ease without her mother's presence.

His breathing was barely discernable. Only by watching his chest rise and fall could she tell that he was alive at all. She looked at the washstand and his personal effects the doctor had laid there. Picking up the letter, she saw the heading. It said 8th Louisiana Volunteer Infantry. So he was from Captain James's regiment! If he had been recently wounded that meant the regiment was engaged at Kernstown. Captain James had not rejoined it yet, so she knew he was safe. But it served as a reminder to her that the war was near and could take friends and loved ones in minutes. She breathed a sigh and felt relieved that her father would be coming home soon.

Finishing the letter, she found it yielded some information about this young man. He was from New Orleans, and was writing his parents to say he expected the regiment to be in a battle soon. He wrote of some friends he had seen from home, and ended with a plea that if he was killed, someone would send the letter on, and notify his family.

Mattie put the letter back with the knife and the money. Her mother came in, and Mattie fidgeted in the chair. "I didn't think I should leave," she fumbled for an excuse.

Moira looked closely at Will. "I don't think he will be waking up soon, but I will bring some soup and tea up." Her Irish roots still told her that tea was the best treatment for any illness. "Then we'll have to get it into him somehow." She turned and left Mattie to muse on the thought that this young soldier was now fighting a battle for his very life.

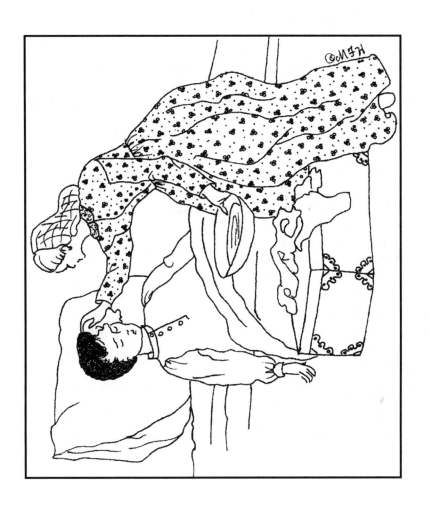

Three days passed and still Will Hamilton slept. Mattie felt she had become an expert at feeding him, even though she had only done it three or four times with a feeding cup and her mother's supervision. She was sitting at the washstand reading, when she looked over to check on him. It was a hot day, and seeing beads of perspiration on his forehead, she took a cloth, wet it, and began to wash his face gently. He had not been shaved, and if he didn't wake up soon, they would have to do that for him too. Slowly, almost unnoticeably, he opened his eyes. Mattie moved back.

"Don't stop," he said weakly. "It feels good."

Mattie was caught off guard. Not that she hadn't realized he might wake up, but it was so unexpected she looked at him as if the furniture had spoken. She found herself staring into the bluest eyes she had ever seen, pale like the color of summer sky. They contrasted sharply with his black hair and brows, making a handsome combination.

"Do I look that bad?" he asked, a little perplexed at the startled look on her face. His voice was faltering, barely a whisper.

"No . . . I'm sorry . . . ," Mattie stammered. "I'm not used to getting any response from you and I was surprised."

A few awkward minutes passed, both of them a little embarrassed. The only girl who had ever seen Will in his nightclothes was his mother. Mattie was very aware that unlike Captain DeCourcey, Will was closer to her own age, not someone you thought of as a father. She felt her cheeks flush.

"How do you feel?" she asked, anything to break the silence.

"Tired, very tired. And sore." He winced as he tried to stir in the bed, pulling his side. "How long have I been here?"

"About three days. But the sergeant who brought you told us that you had lain on the field for hours."

"That would be the cavalrymen who found me. I was lucky they came along."

"So you remember that? Coming here?" asked Mattie.

"Just barely. I remember they changed my jacket, because my own was soaked." With blood, he thought but didn't say.

"Yes, we thought you were in the cavalry, until the doctor found your letter and told us you were with the 8th Louisiana. I know a captain with the 8th. Captain James DeCourcey. Do you know him?" Mattie was glad they had found a common thread to break the awkward moment of meeting.

"Yes, he is my captain. He was wounded back in May. We knew he was staying near here. Is this where? Are you the folks who tended him?" His voice showed his surprise at such a coincidence.

"No, our neighbors the Adamses did. He rejoins his regiment any day now."

Moira walked in to find two young people having a most enjoyable conversation. She had brought the usual tray of tea and broth.

"Well, what have we here?" she said, obvious surprise and satisfaction showing in her voice. "It's good to see you awake. I hope you are hungry enough to eat something."

"Yes, ma'am, I think so."

"Well, I'll let you get started on this with Mattie's help, and I'll go back downstairs and find something more substantial than this liquid diet. Then maybe we can get you shaved."

By the end of the day, Will Hamilton was back in the land of the living, on a long road to recovery.

CHAPTER FIVE

Sergeant Andrew MacDonald stopped in the shade of the huge oak tree beside the Valley Pike. He leaned his rifle against the tree and took off his hat. Wiping the sweat from his brow and running his hand through his thick auburn hair, he readjusted his slouch hat. He took his canteen and had a drink of the cool water he had gotten at the Miller's well. He was almost home, having walked ten miles just that morning. It was almost noon. He decided to sit down and take a short rest, as it was so cool there under the big tree. All was quiet around him, no traffic on the road, none of his comrades with their usual banter and camp noises. He was so anxious to get home, after not seeing his wife and daughter for six months. But news from comrades coming and going had kept him in touch, so he knew all was well with the family. The past few months this part of the Valley had been full of Yankee troops under the command of General David Hunter, plundering and burning farms and houses. He thought about Moira. They had left Ireland together as young newlyweds and come across the Atlantic to Virginia more than sixteen years ago. He had a brother who had come here earlier, and convinced Andrew to make this Valley his home too. There were many similarities to his native land and he felt at ease, except for the summer heat. That he didn't think he would ever adjust to. He was now thirty-eight years old, with a fine farm. He hoped it would survive this war.

He found he couldn't relax, so decided to press on and go the extra three miles home before the August heat increased. He picked up his rifle just as he heard a horse clip-clopping along at a trot behind him, heading south. He turned and started to walk along the side of the road as the rider drew near. Andrew recognized the uniform of a Confederate officer and breathed a sigh of relief. The rider slowed and Andrew saluted.

"Sergeant MacDonald? It is my pleasure to meet you," said Captain DeCourcey.

"Captain," Andrew nodded politely, "I am curious as to how you know me. I don't recall meeting you, Sir."

"Forgive me, I will explain. My name is Captain James DeCourcey of the 8th Louisiana."

"Well!" Andrew smiled in recognition. "Moira and Mattie have told me all about you in their letters. You stayed with the Adams family. It's a pleasure to meet you, Sir!" Andrew extended his hand and Captain DeCourcey shook it heartily.

"You have a very fine family, Sergeant," he said. "They eagerly await your arrival. As for myself, I am on my way to join my regiment."

"Well, you'll find them camped about twenty miles yonder way," and Andrew pointed south up the Valley toward Strasburg.

"I am much obliged," said Captain DeCourcey. "I hope we meet again, Sergeant." He squeezed his horse back into a trot. Riding down the road before they lost sight of each other, he turned and waved a final good-bye.

Andrew walked at the easy gait a man acquires after being a foot soldier in many campaigns, his rifle sitting at an angle on his shoulder. He saw his farm in the distance, and quickened his pace.

CHAPTER SIX

Private William Hamilton had been at the MacDonald farm for a week now. Although he was still in bed, too weak to do more than sit up for a few minutes at a time, his youth was making his recovery progress rapidly.

Moira came into the room with his dinner, followed by Mattie.

"We've something very special for you today, Will," said Moira. They had become familiar enough with him to call him by his first name, accepting him as a temporary family member. He smiled at them both.

"You both are spoiling me rotten," he laughed. "My mother would be glad to know I'm so well cared for."

"Jenna made you a special treat. Apple pie!" Moira uncovered the dishes on the tray. All the attention and good food he had received were the reasons he had survived and he was well aware of it.

"That's my favorite! Be sure and thank her for me, will you?" He was genuinely touched.

"I will. Now, Mattie, if you will help Will with his dinner, I'll go back down and help Jenna air the mattresses. There's also comforters to mend." She looked at Mattie, reminding her that was her job.

"Yes, ma'am." Mattie was glad her mother was leaving. She enjoyed Will's company. She had been sitting in his room, reading to him in the afternoons to break up the monotony of his confinement to bed. She learned that he was also Irish, which made him a special pet in her mother's eyes. Although he had been born in Louisiana, his parents had come over from Ireland like the MacDonalds.

Mattie pulled up a chair and balanced the tray on her lap to serve as a table. Will was able to feed himself, but not strong enough to get up.

"How are you feeling today?" she asked, handing him a plate of ham and vegetables. Will nodded as he chewed a mouthful of ham.

"Much better. Still sore, but a little stronger."

She handed him a glass of buttermilk. He took a sip and gave it back.

"I'm looking forward to hearing what happens to Ivanhoe in that tournament," he smiled. Mattie had been reading him the book, and they were both caught up in the story of the brave knight and his lady Rowena. Mattie liked the romance, and Will being a soldier could identify with the war between Saxon and Norman.

"I am too," she said eagerly. "I only have to help mama for a little while, then I'll be up. Maybe you should take a nap while I'm doing my chores." Will finished the last of his dinner, and lay back on the pillows. There was a breeze blowing in the window by the bed and it seemed a little cooler than the previous day. Mattie took the tray and rose to leave.

"I promise, I'll be back as soon as I can." She glanced out the window and her body froze. Then her face broke into a gaping smile, and she almost dropped the tray.

"It's Papa! My father's home!"

In the yard below, Andrew MacDonald was greeted by his wife with a hug. Mattie watched from the window as her parents locked in an embrace, her mother beside herself with emotion, kissing her father. Putting their arms around one another's waist, they walked out of sight beneath the porch roof. "I'll be back, Will!" Mattie called over her shoulder as she raced out the door, almost tripping in her haste.

Will smiled and nestled his head in the pillow. He listened to the happy sounds of a soldier's homecoming in the rooms below. He thought of his own parents and the pangs of homesickness made a lump in his throat. Swallowing hard, he closed his eyes to the tears that were welling up.

CHAPTER SEVEN

"Papa!" Mattie bounded down the stairs. Her parents stood in the hallway, their arms still around each other. Jenna was there too, her brown face beaming at them. She took the tray as Mattie landed on the last step.

"Miss Mattie, you go break yo neck, and all these dishes too!" she scolded.

Her father hugged her tight. "Hello, lass," he said. She breathed deeply, catching the familiar smell of him as they stood close for a moment.

"I'm so glad you're home. We have someone for you to meet!" she said excitedly. Andrew smiled curiously. Moira suddenly realized he knew nothing about their patient. She put her hands to her face.

"Oh, I forgot, you don't know about Will."

"Will?" asked Andrew puzzled.

"I'll tell you all about him. For now you need to rest and eat." Moira began her fussing, taking his hat, and blanket roll, leaning the musket beside the door.

She helped him out of his jacket and hung it on the halltree.

"I'll get Mr. Andrew's dinner ready," said Jenna, just as fussy as Moira. Then they all went through the breezeway into the summer kitchen, where Jenna had the little table set and the food ready.

Andrew ate heartily, although he was tired. It was the first real meal he had eaten at a table in months. He was glad to be home. While they ate, he was plied with questions about the war, and the battle of the week before. He related all the news of friends in the army, and told of his meeting Captain DeCourcey on the road.

"A real gentleman, I could see that," he said. "His regiment took a mauling the day he was wounded, at that Mule Shoe at Spotsylvania. Heavy casualties. One thing we all agree on—those Tigers are crack troops. They're never beaten." He told of the admiration all soldiers felt for the men from Louisiana.

"Well, I guess we'd better tell you; we have a Tiger of our own upstairs," said Moira. She and Mattie told him of the young soldier they had rescued. He could see the fondness they had acquired for Private William Hamilton.

"I look forward to meeting the young man," said Andrew. Then with a seriousness he added, "I'm glad you helped him. I've seen so many men suffer, and the rest of us feel so helpless, because there's nothing we can do."

"I would hope that if it were you out there—" Moira's voice cracked, "well that someone would take you in and do the same," she finished. "I've still got mattresses to air," she changed to a lighter subject. "Mattie, why don't you take your father upstairs and introduce him to Will."

Mattie was delighted. They went upstairs together. She wanted her father to like Will as much as she and her mother did. They quietly opened the door. Will was dozing, but was aware of them.

"Let's don't disturb him now." He heard another man's voice with the same Irish brogue as his own father's.

"I'm not asleep, please come in." Will sounded insistent, and Andrew and Mattie came in. Andrew walked over to the bed and extended a friendly hand. He could see why the women liked Will. He was a strikingly handsome boy. "Pleased to meet you lad," he said. "I was at Kernstown, where you were wounded. Fierce fighting it was. You're lucky to be alive. How is the wound?"

"I'll mend, thanks to your nurses here," Will smiled.

They began to talk about the war, and Andrew seated himself in the chair beside the bed. Mattie smiled at their immediate rapport. She left them to get acquainted, returning to help her mother with the bedding. She knew they would not find out the fate of Ivanhoe this afternoon. It would have to wait.

CHAPTER EIGHT

"My parents were lowland Scots—descended from those who came to the north of Ireland to escape English rule. So I guess I'm really good Scottish stock. Then Moira and I came here before Matilda was born." Andrew MacDonald was proud of his ancestry, and he had embraced the Cause of his new homeland.

"I suppose we Scots are destined to be a warrior tribe, against any tyrannous rule." He laughed at the historical perspective.

"The same with my Irish forefathers. It seems we'll never stop fighting the English," Will added. "I consider myself a son of Louisiana. I was born there." Then both men became silent, and Andrew spoke with seriousness.

"The war is taking a heavy toll in good men. And the Yankees seem to be reinforced daily. I'm concerned about Virginia if our army is pushed out of this Valley. Hunter almost succeeded this summer." Andrew looked out the window as if seeing something far beyond the view of mountain ridges to the west. He looked back at the boy sitting up in bed. "I'm glad you're here with my family."

"I'm afraid I'm not worth much under the circumstances," Will said modestly.

The nine days that Andrew was home were filled with much happiness. The war was put as far aside as it was possible to put aside a storm outside one's door, and the evenings were marked with singing in the parlor, and lively conversation. With Andrew's help, Will had gotten to his feet and felt well enough to come down and join them. Now, on Andrew's last night home, they sat in the parlor, singing Irish songs of the past and patriotic songs of their South. Will had a fairly good voice, and he and Andrew joined in a rendition of "Eileen Aroon," accompanied by Moira on the piano forte. The sorrowful ballad ended the entertainment on a somber note.

"Well, I do believe we've tired Private Hamilton out enough for one night," said Moira. Will smiled. He was tired, but would not have missed this evening for anything.

"No Yankee bullet can stop an Irishman from his singing," he said, jokingly. They all laughed, a much needed antidote to the somber mood.

Andrew helped Will back upstairs, while Moira and Mattie tidied and straightened the parlor. Jenna took the dishes from their evening tea back to the kitchen, and they prepared for bed.

Later, Mattie sat at her dressing table, combing out the long blonde tendrils of her hair. She thought about her father's leaving on the morrow, and about the conversations she had overheard between him and Will. The concern in their voices made her sense that the South was being hard pressed. She reflected on the evening.

Sitting and crocheting a collar, listening to the men talk about the war, and army life, and musing on "what ifs" for the future, she had found herself watching Will. Now on his feet, he seemed more like a man than a boy. He was wise beyond his years, the experience of survival had done that. He had a smile that Mattie found irresistible, and she liked watching him when he wasn't conscious of it. She looked at her own face in the mirror, playing with her hair to see how she might make herself look older than her fifteen years.

The next day the cavalryman who had brought Will there returned.

"We thought the young man might want these," said the sergeant when Moira answered his knock at the door. He handed her Will's musket and his uniform jacket.

"Glad to hear he's recovering. He was mighty low that day."

"Thank you," said Moira as she took the jacket. "I'm sure he'll be glad to know these weren't lost." She admired the blue jacket, its elaborate and ornate style so different from that worn by the Virginia troops.

"Would you come in and refresh yourself? I can get you a cold glass of buttermilk."

"I'd like that ma'am, if it's no trouble." He seemed so grateful for the respite from the heat that Moira brought him a ham biscuit as an added treat. It was just passed noon, and since Andrew hadn't left yet, he joined the sergeant.

They sat in the cool parlor, the cavalryman taking his hat off and relaxing. Careful to keep his spurs a good distance from the chair's upholstery, he crossed his legs.

"What regiment are you with, Sergeant?" he asked Andrew.

"The 33rd Virginia Infantry. I've been home on a furlough. Got home just after Kernstown. Are things still quiet?"

The sergeant nodded. "General Early's still planning on staying in the Valley and keeping the Yankees from reinforcing Grant across the mountains. But I understand General Lee's having a hard time, fighting a defensive action against more than twice his number. We may have to send some troops back over to him." The sergeant sipped his buttermilk as if it were wine, relishing every drink and taking his time, making it last. "How's that young Tiger upstairs?" he inquired about Will. "Getting stronger everyday. Recovering quite nicely. But I'm afraid he'll be out of action for at least another month."

"I'm glad your wife took him in. The hospital was so crowded he would have died if I'd left him there, I know he would." He munched on his biscuit thoughtfully.

"I'll tell you, those men from Louisiana are about the toughest fighters I've ever seen. I'm sure glad they're on our side so I don't have to fight 'em. Were you at Kernstown?"

"Yes, I saw their charge," Andrew's voice became excited at the memory. "They pushed them all the way back to the state line." Both men laughed. He acknowledged the bravery of these fierce fighters, exiled from their homes, keeping his own free.

"His regiment is still here in the Valley with Early. He's keepin' 'em busy. They may go back to reinforce General Lee."

The sergeant finished his biscuit, rose and picked up his hat.

"Well, I just stopped by to bring him his gun and jacket. They laundered it at the hospital for him. Managed to get the blood stains out. I thought he might be tired of being mistaken for a Virginia Cavalier." They both chuckled.

Andrew walked out on the porch with the sergeant. They shook hands.

"Pleased to meet you. Take care, and thank your wife. I'm obliged for the refreshment."

"Good luck," said Andrew, as the trooper mounted his horse. Looking back and waving, he urged his mount into a trot toward the Valley Pike.

Andrew leaned against the porch column. He gazed at the mountains that stood to the south, the conical shape of Fisher's Hill rising up from the Valley floor. Like protecting sentinels they had sheltered this Valley for three years, and hidden the gray-clad soldiers fighting for her. Somewhere near Strasburg his regiment waited. He would wait for the heat of the day to pass before he shouldered his rifle and accoutrements of war and returned to the life of a soldier.

CHAPTER NINE

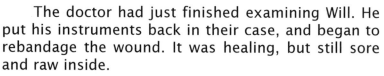

The doctor had just finished examining Will. He put his instruments back in their case, and began to rebandage the wound. It was healing, but still sore and raw inside.

"You're doing fine, young man," said Dr. Johnson, his white drooping mustache wriggling beneath his nose. "I suggest you try to get up more, get a little exercise before you get any weaker. Just don't be up and down the stairs too many times."

"Yes, Sir," Will agreed. He had seen his wound each time the bandage was changed, first by Mrs. MacDonald, then Dr. Johnson. It had left his side mangled, the new scar tissue would be a reminder for the rest of his life of that day at Kernstown.

He had played the scene out in his mind over and over, seeing himself running forward in a charge, surrounded by comrades yelling, the scent of battle heavy with powder smoke and sweat. Then suddenly he had felt a blow that spun him around and knocked him to the ground. Slipping into unconsciousness, he had apparently been overlooked by any one searching for wounded until the cavalrymen came by and found him.

After Dr. Johnson was finished, Will sat on the side of the bed. He pulled his shirt over his head, slowly, and reached for a pair of gray trousers Mrs. MacDonald had found for him. Altering them, she managed to make them fit his slender frame fairly well. He pulled them on, and stood, adjusting the suspenders.

"How long have you been in the army, son?" asked Dr. Johnson, making conversation as he prepared to leave.

"Two years, Sir. I left Louisiana just as the Yankees occupied New Orleans. I was too young to go with the first of my regiment in 1861."

"How old are you now?" asked the doctor.

"Just turned nineteen this summer." Will smiled. "One month before I got this." He gestured at his bandaged side.

Dr. Johnson walked toward the door, sadly contemplating the youthful valor the war was swallowing up. He was met by Mattie and Moira.

"I'll be back to check on him in a week or so. I've still got patients at the hospital to tend. He's coming along nicely." He looked at Will and waved a good-bye. "Ladies," he said as he touched his hat, "I'll see my way out."

"Good-bye, Dr. Johnson," said Moira.

Will was standing by the bed, a little uncertainly. He noticed they were both smiling sheepishly, Mattie holding something behind her back. Then mother and daughter exchanged looks.

"Why don't you tell him," said Moira to Mattie. Mattie looked from her mother to Will, then walked forward.

"We have a surprise for you," she said. "Close your eyes."

Will looked puzzled, his brows knit over his eyes. But he did as he was told. Mattie brought the short Zouave jacket from behind her back. Unfolding it, she held it up in front of him.

"You can look now," she said.

Will opened his eyes to see the uniform jacket he had thought was surely lost forever. "I can't believe it," he said, obviously pleased, and took it. The bright red braid was all intact, the blue wool cleaned of the blood and dirt of battle. "The cavalryman saved it for you. He said they cleaned it at the hospital. Your musket's here too."

Will turned to the washstand mirror and slipped his coat on. Mattie saw the transformation from wounded boy to soldier as he adjusted the fit, turning in front of the mirror to admire himself. Then he saw the tear on the right side, caused by the bullet. Mrs. MacDonald had already noticed.

"I'm certain I can mend that," she said unconcerned. "My, Will, you look handsome."

Mattie thought the same thing. The short, French-style jacket seemed to add a dash to Will with its brilliant red braid and foreign style. He made an impressive figure, although the elegance of the jacket made the gray pants look homely.

"I wore out the trousers last year. With the occupation, most of my regiment have lost their original uniforms like this one, and wear regular gray shell jackets. They will be envious that I've still got mine," he smiled, still admiring his return to something resembling a soldier.

"Would you like to come and sit downstairs?" asked Moira. "Mattie, why don't you keep Will company in the parlor for awhile. It's much cooler down there than up here."

"That would be a pleasure ma'am," said Will. He was tired of being confined to bed, even though his side was still sore. He followed the women through the door and moving gingerly, down the stairs. Moira went back to the kitchen to help Jenna.

"I thought we could read some more of *Ivanhoe*," said Mattie, looking over her shoulder at Will as he took the steps slowly. Once in the parlor, Will sat on the sofa, while Mattie sat across from him in a chair, the open book resting in her palms.

All eyes were turned to see the new champion which these sounds announced, and no sooner were the barriers opened than he paced into the lists. As far as could be judged of a man sheathed in armour, the new adventurer did not greatly exceed the middle size, and seemed to be rather slender than strongly made.... He was mounted on a gallant black horse...the dexterity with which he managed his steed, and something of youthful grace which he displayed in his manner, won him the favor of the multitude.

"Look, Will, there's a drawing," Mattie said, and came to sit down next to him. "It's Ivanhoe, although the spectators at the tournament don't know that yet."

Will showed interest in the drawing, studying the armour and weapons. They sat with their heads together over the book.

"I'd like to have some armour like that against those Yankee bullets," he laughed. "But I don't think even that would stop them."

Mattie's heart quickened at being so close to him, their shoulders touching as they discussed the picture of the knight. The parallel strife of the Norman-Saxon conflict of old in the story, and the present struggle of the South were so similar, both Mattie and Will burned with enthusiasm for the Saxon Cause represented by Ivanhoe, and loathed the injustice of the Normans. More than that, the feelings of the knight for his lady, and Rowena's own unspoken

affection, represented their unspoken feelings for each other.

The story drew them together, as the days passed, and they sat in the parlor, Mattie patiently reading while Will listened. The Holy Cause of the Saxons was their Holy Cause for Independence. The tournaments were their nearby battlefields, and the chivalrous knights donned Confederate gray.

And Will Hamilton became Mattie's Ivanhoe.

CHAPTER TEN

One afternoon, as they sat in the parlor, Mattie and Will were interrupted by the sounds of an approaching buggy on the drive. The voice of a woman was heard indistinctly. Mattie went to the window and drawing back the lace curtain, recognized Mrs. Dawson from town. She and her husband owned the millinery shop, and their daughter Emmaline was Mattie's age. She didn't think of Emmaline as a best friend, but they got along. She tended to talk too much and was always asking too many questions, becoming downright annoying after awhile. Before the war, they saw each other at social occasions and school, but that was before the war. There were very few social occasions anymore.

Mattie heard her mother in the hall, greeting them at the door.

"It's the Dawsons," said Mattie, making an unpleasant face. "Now we'll get to listen to Emmaline rattle on. Maybe they won't stay very long," she added hopefully.

Will had walked over to stand behind her, looking over her head at the guests, now on the porch. Mattie relished his nearness, but her thoughts were interrupted by her mother's appearance in the parlor doorway, accompanied by the Dawsons.

"Mattie, we have company," said her mother. She and Mrs. Dawson were happy to see one another. The loneliness of living out on the farm always made Moira welcome any company, especially another woman.

"Mrs. Dawson and Emmaline, I would like for you to meet Private William Hamilton. He's staying with us while recovering from a wound he received at Kernstown." Mattie watched the two sizing Will up with their eyes, as if he were so different from anything they had ever seen before.

"Good afternoon, ladies," he said as he took a stiff bow. His side wouldn't allow that much movement. He felt awkward around all these women and girls, wishing for the comfort of male company in an army camp. But he didn't want to appear rude.

"Well, let's all sit down and I'll have Jenna bring some lemonade."

"That would be wonderful," said Mrs. Dawson, arranging her hoop skirts in a chair. She wore a stylish new hat, a trapping of her status as the millinery owner. Will preferred a single chair, and Mattie and Emmaline sat together on the sofa. Moira left, leaving Mattie as the go-between for the guests. But she knew there would be no lack of conversation with the Dawsons.

"Well, Private Hamilton, what regiment are you with?" asked Mrs. Dawson.

"The 8th Louisiana Infantry, ma'am," answered Will proudly.

"Oh," said Mrs. Dawson, a hint of disappointment in her voice. "Louisiana Tigers I presume?"

"Yes, ma'am. It seems all we Louisiana troops have been lumped together as Tigers. They were only a company. There's not many of that original band left now. Most of them have been killed here in Virginia." He said it with a cutting edge in his voice. Some Virginians had come to regard the Tigers as an inferior lot of undisciplined pirates. And there had been incidents in some of the regiments that Will was not proud of. But the 8th was made up of good men. Captain DeCourcey was a gentleman and always kept his company in line. The fact that so many had died for this state should have bought some kind of salvation for their boisterous behavior. He defended his comrades.

"I myself am honored to serve with men of such a reputation as fighters."

He was aware that he also owed a lot to people like the MacDonalds and the Virginia cavalryman who had found him. He softened his tone and smiled.

"I am very thankful for all the care and attention my comrades and I have had, here and at the hospital in town."

Mrs. Dawson smiled. Perhaps she had judged too harshly. This young man was obviously well mannered. She had heard about the Tigers's reputation as rather free spirits, but after working in the hospital at Mrs. Nisewander's, she knew they were admired by the soldiers and had been the reason for the victory at Kernstown.

"Where are you from in Louisiana?" she asked.

"New Orleans. My father works as head clerk for a shipping company down by the docks." Unlike the prevalent view that most Louisianians were planters like Captain DeCourcey, Will knew very few men of the 8th who owned even one slave.

Moira returned with the lemonade. Mattie was becoming impatient with the whole situation and decided

she would rather be some place else. Emmaline had been glancing at Will every few seconds, and Mattie wished he had his Zouave jacket on so she could see how handsome and dashing he looked. It was late August and the heat was too intense for wearing a wool jacket outside military orders, so Will was only wearing his shirt and the trousers her mother had altered. He looked more like a plowboy than a soldier in those clothes.

"Emmaline, let's go sit on the porch," whispered Mattie.

"Alright," said Emmaline, expecting Will to accompany them.

"Mother, may we be excused?" asked Mattie.

With their mothers' permission they took their lemonade outside. The porch was still too hot, so Mattie suggested they go around the side of the house to the big oak tree by the kitchen. The girls plopped down on the cool grass, their legs gathered up under their hoopskirts.

"Isn't he coming too?" asked Emmaline, craning her neck to see around the corner of the house.

"Probably not. He's only been able to get out of bed for a week. He had a terrible wound." Mattie liked having the air of authority she could use when telling Emmaline all about Will's wound and how she and her mother had nursed him. Emmaline seemed awestruck and listened intently to the details.

"I wish we had a soldier to care for," she whined. "There have been so many families in Newtown who did. Do you know Amanda Osbourne? They have one who was wounded in the head." She said it in a bragging way, as if it were her own personal accomplishment. "But most of them go to the hospital at Mrs. Nisewander's boardinghouse if they stay in town." She absently sipped her lemonade. "He's very good looking, Mattie. How old is he?"

"Nineteen," said Mattie. She felt jealous, some-what to her surprise.

"Does he have a sweetheart back in New Orleans?

He probably does," Emmaline said, still trying to see around the corner of the house, hoping Will would appear.

The thought left Mattie speechless. She realized how little she knew about Will. What if he did have a girl at home? He had never said so, but then again, no one had ever asked. It made her feel depressed. The intimate contact necessary between them in caring for his wound had put them in a situation far different from that experienced socially. She had come to think of him as "her" soldier and had given no concern to the fact that he would be leaving once he was well, and she would never see him again. She forced the disturbing thought from her mind, not wanting to face it in front of Emmaline. "I don't think so. As a matter of fact, I know he doesn't," she said with more certainty than she felt.

They heard the back door slam, and their mothers came out. Mrs. MacDonald had a concerned look on her face, and called Jenna. Will followed them, his first venture outside since he had been brought here. Mrs. Dawson called Emmaline.

"We must go Moira, but I thought I'd better warn you, so you can be prepared. You remember all the terrible things that happened in Newtown with Hunter's troops." Mrs. Dawson frowned at the memory.

"Thank you, I'm grateful for the thought Betsy." Moira looked sad and distraught.

"Emmaline, time to go, dear!" called her mother more insistently.

Emmaline and Mattie rose and walked toward their mothers. Will stood on the porch, looking around the farm.

"Good-bye, Private Hamilton. I hope you recover soon." She said it with sincerity. Will smiled and nodded a good-bye.

"Thank you, ma'am," he said politely.

The Dawsons left, Emmaline still glancing back at Will as they walked around the corner of the house. He appeared not to notice. Mattie watched her mother, who had come down the back steps and was searching the backyard with her eyes as if she was trying to remember where treasure was buried. Will slowly came down the steps to stand beside her.

"Mattie, we've got work to do," said Moira.

"If you're thinking of burying anything here, it won't do any good. The fresh turned earth will give it away." Will sounded sure of himself.

Moira looked at him, realizing he was right. She spoke to Mattie.

"Mrs. Dawson came by to say there have been Yankee troops seen in the north end of the county. They're some of Sheridan's men." She spoke with the voice of someone trying to stay calm but fighting fear.

"We need to hide all the meats and get the livestock moved. If they come here, they'll surely steal it all." Now she began to sound determined. "I simply won't let them take everything we've worked so hard to prepare and raise." She thought a minute.

"Will, if you feel up to it, you and Mattie can take the cows down to the woods, by the creek. It's over behind the Adams's place. I'll get Jenna and we'll find someway to hide the silver and food.

"But Mother, there's Confederate troops not far from here. Why would Yankees come this far?" Mattie couldn't make sense of all the panic.

"The troops are all the way down at Martinsburg. They're not in the Upper Valley anymore. And your father said General Early may have to send men over to General Lee. The only troops we can count on here are Mosby's men. Now get the cows and take your time to make sure they're far enough out of sight in the woods."

"I'll help you, Mattie," said Will.

"Are you sure you're up to it, lad?" asked Moira. "You've only been on your feet a week."

"I'll manage," said Will.

Mattie changed quickly into a plain skirt and boots. She joined Will and they turned the four milk cows out of the barn lot. Because Will was still weak, they took Dandy, the carriage horse, and put a bridle on him so Will could ride. Then they started with the cows, Mattie driving them with a long stick on one side, while Will rode on the other. It was about two miles to the creek that ran between their field and the Adamses' field, and there was an old stockpen that had not been used for a long time.

"What do you think the Yankees will do if they come?" asked Mattie. She tried not to sound afraid.

Will shook his head. "I don't know, Mattie. I was in New Orleans when they first occupied it. They destroyed a lot of property, wanton destruction—totally unnecessary. And they were rude to people on the street, treating women like common criminals. It's the reason I left to fight."

Mattie's mind raced, trying to create a scene of what to expect and how to cope with it. Will continued.

"They would go in stores and take merchandise and just toss it in the street. It wasn't like they took what they needed. They simply destroyed it so no one else could use it." His face was stern, his blue eyes cold. "If they do come, the best thing is just not to let them see anything you have, and hope they're in a hurry so they'll leave soon."

Suddenly Mattie felt panic cut her breath short. "Will! What about you? What will they do to you?" she asked, reaching out with the stick to tap one cow who had slowed to a stop. The beast leaped forward, shaking her horned head in defiance. Mattie walked quickly, trying to keep up with the cows and Will.

He had not given any thought to himself. He and Mattie looked at one another as it dawned on them that the Yankees may take him as a prisoner of war. Neither spoke for a few minutes.

"Oh, Will, we'll have to hide you too," said Mattie, the concern for his safety showing in her voice.

Will thought as they kept moving. "I suppose I'll have to do something to keep them from knowing who I am. Maybe they'll think I'm your brother who didn't join the army." But even as he said it, he knew that would be no excuse. He was of military age, and that would be enough for the Yankees to take him. He searched his mind for some idea of how to elude them and prevent them knowing he was a wounded Confederate soldier. They hurried the cows on, the creek and stockpen now in sight. When they reached the stockpen, they drove the cows in, and discovered some of the fence rails were off and needed repair. As it was a rail fence, most of the rails lay strewn about. Will slid carefully off the horse.

"We need to put these rails back up and be sure they can't get out. Little good it will do us to bring them here if the Yankees catch them wandering around later."

Will lifted a rail in the middle, crouching down to keep from bending his side. Mattie watched as he picked it up, rose, and began to lift it on top of the others. Halfway up, he hesitated. Instantly, he went down on one knee, dropping the rail, his face distorted in pain.

"I can't do it, Mattie," he said, his voice betraying the pain and frustration at his unfitness.

Mattie went and knelt beside him. "I'll help you, Will," she said sympathetically, as she picked up one end. It was very heavy. After a moment, Will got to his feet, and by taking one end together, they lifted all the rails back on top of the fence. Will leaned against the fence, folding his arms on the top rail and burying his face in them. Mattie couldn't see his face but she was sure he was crying.

"I'll get the horse," she said. She ran and caught the gelding and looking around, discovered a stump that was fairly tall and that Will could use as a mounting block. "Will!" she called. "Look, you can stand here to mount."

He had straightened up, but he looked pale, leaning with his back against the fence. He looked at Mattie standing there, holding the horse. He had felt the sharp pain in his side and knew the wound was bleeding again, but he had to get back to the house, and get Mattie safe. Summoning all the strength he could muster, he walked to the stump, climbing up and finally mounting the horse. Mattie could see that he was in pain. "Just rest, Will. I'll lead Dandy home." He nodded, slumping slightly forward. One hand held his side while the other clutched a fist full of mane. Mattie led Dandy at a slow walk all the way home.

CHAPTER ELEVEN

They reached the barnyard, but Mattie led Dandy past it and up to the back door of the house. Will had not said a word the whole time, although he was still sitting up. She saw her mother and Jenna amid a flurry of activity, gathering goods from the smokehouse; silverware and the tea set she had brought from Ireland, had been retrieved from the dining room. Jenna was taking them into her little house which adjoined the kitchen. The whole scene started to impress upon Mattie the urgency of the situation. Her mother looked up at their approach. She started to reprimand Mattie about dawdling so long.

"Mattie, why—" Upon seeing Will, she stopped in mid-thought. "Oh, mother in heaven," she mumbled as she dropped two jars of apple butter she was holding and looked intently at Will, then dashed to the horse's side.

"Mattie, get the horse as close to the porch steps as you can."

They maneuvered the patient gelding over, and he stood quietly. Mattie was frightened by the look on her mother's face and the alarm in her voice.

"Will, can you get down?" Moira asked him in a firm voice.

Then Mattie looked at Will. He had a strange stare in his eyes, and his teeth were clenched. She had not been aware of what had happened, she was busy leading Dandy. Then she saw the blood. It had seeped through his shirt, streaming through his fingers as he held his side, and dripped down the horse's shoulder. Mattie was horrified that he was bleeding to death, so much was there.

"Mattie, help me," said her mother, as she pulled Will gently off the horse by the arm, catching his shoulders by standing on the top step. He managed to find his feet and by stumbling with Mattie under one arm and Moira under the other, they got him upstairs.

He sat on the side of the bed as Moira pulled his shirt off. "I felt it start bleeding again," he said, his voice trembling, "when we started to fix the rails."

Moira was concerned that he would go into shock, but he only seemed very weak. "You never should have done all that in your condition. You're not healed deep inside yet," she scolded no one in particular. Mattie had brought a pitcher of water and poured it in the basin. She had clean bandages ready, and Moira was undoing the old bloody one. They looked at the wound. It was definitely irritated from the strenuous work, and had bled a good deal, but it was beginning to clot now. Moira cleaned it and repacked it with lint, working swiftly.

"We got the cows in the pen and fixed all the rails," said Will. "They should be safe. But someone will have to go down and turn them out to graze and milk them everyday."

"Jenna is burying what she can in her quarters under the floorboards. We hope they won't think to look in her rooms. We turned the pigs loose, they'll go to the woods on their own." Moira talked as she rebandaged Will. "Maybe we'll be lucky and they won't come this far below Winchester. Ours is one of the few farms they didn't raid before when Hunter came through back in June. That was when they stole the Adamses' horse." She was finished with the bandage and tied a neat knot to hold it tight. Then she got a clean shirt for Will and helped him put it on. He seemed more steady now, but he was still very pale.

"There, young man, you just lie down and rest. I'll get you some supper. Whatever you do, don't get up."

Will was too tired to argue. He lay down gratefully. Moira took the bloody shirt and went back downstairs to help Jenna hide the rest of their provisions.

"I'm sorry," said Mattie.

"It's not your fault," said Will as he looked at her and smiled. "We had to do what had to be done. I know what to expect from the Yankee army." He spoke with the assurance of someone aware of what was at stake. He studied the ceiling for a moment.

"Bring my musket up here, Mattie," he said. He looked around the room, as a man searches for a defensive position. "My cartridge box was on me when I came here wasn't it?" He had no need to be concerned with his equipment before now.

"Yes," Mattie remembered. "We put all your things in here." She quickly crossed the room to the huge armoire and opened the door, taking out his cartridge box, haversack and jacket. She draped the jacket over a chair.

"Excellent," said Will from the bed. Mattie brought the accoutrements to him. He eagerly opened the cartridge box to find it almost full—thirty rounds.

"Good thing those boys in blue ran that day, I didn't have to fire many rounds."

"I'll go down and get the gun," and she hurried down the stairs. It was in the hall, leaning against the corner where her father had left it. She grabbed the long Enfield musket with both hands and awkwardly started back up the stairs. The gun was heavy and she was out of breath from the effort by the time she reached Will's room.

"Good girl," he rewarded her. "I guess it's time for Ivanhoe to prepare for the tournament," he smiled a tired, pale smile as he inspected the musket. The ramrod was there and Andrew had cleaned the gun before he left. Will laid it on the bed beside him, with the cartridge box.

"You had better get some rest now," said Mattie. "I'll be back in a little while." She closed the door and on second thought looked back in. Will lay with his eyes closed. They had worked together as a team that day, united by the common cause of survival. She would not let the Yankees take him. She loved him too much.

With a determined set in her jaw, she closed the door softly and went downstairs to help prepare her home against the ravages of an invading army.

CHAPTER TWELVE

Mattie went downstairs and out to the kitchen. Jenna had fixed Will a plate and Moira sat at the table, a worried look on her face, leaning on her hand. The kitchen had been stripped bare of all foodstuffs and provisions except for several days' worth stored on the shelves and tables. It looked as if the Yankees had already been here.

"We'll have to decide about feeding the stock that are loose, and one of us will have to go down and tend the cows. We may have to do this for a while, until we know the Yankees are gone."

Jenna set a plate of food in front of Moira. "Don't worry now, we'll tend to things. You jes eat," Jenna ordered. "Miz Mattie, you set down, I got yore's here too." Mattie sat down mechanically, her mind on other matters.

"What about Will, Mother. We can't let them find him."

Her mother picked at the food distractedly. "I've thought of that too, Mattie." She sighed. "If only his wound hadn't reopened—," she dropped the fork and covered her eyes with one hand. "I don't know what to do, but we'll think of something."

Mattie had no appetite at all. They all three sat at the table in silence, too preoccupied to eat.

"I'm not very hungry. I think I'll take Will's supper up and sit with him a little while." Mattie rose and picked up the plate.

"I wish I had acquired a man on this farm before your father left. With just us women, it's too hard to manage under these circumstances." Moira was on the verge of tears. For over three years the stress of living in a war-torn country had worn her down. Not only did she have a husband away, risking his life, but she had a daughter and a farm here to protect. Her endurance was reaching the breaking point. She fought the tears. Mattie came over and put an arm around her mother's shoulders.

"It will be alright, Mother. I know it will." It seemed to help. Her mother nodded in agreement. "I'm just very tired. But Jenna and I have settled everything. Now the only thing left to do is wait." She got up, leaving her food untouched and went outside in the growing dusk. She stood for a long time looking north, straining her ears for sounds. Jenna came over to Mattie and hugged her shoulders.

"Yore mama jest tired, honey. If the Yankees come we jes do de bes' we can and de good Lord will tek care of de res'."

Mattie smiled at Jenna. Dear sweet Jenna. What would she do without her? She had always made Mattie feel better.

Mattie took the plate of food upstairs and listened outside Will's door. There was no sound, and she opened the door softly and entered. It was just past dusk, the light coming through the west window. The room was washed in the twilight, the lamp not having been lit, so Will must be asleep. Setting the plate on the washstand, Mattie leaned over the bed. He was sound asleep, his hand resting on the musket by his side. She listened to his steady breathing for a moment. He looked even more youthful than he was, lying in the half-light.

"I won't let anything happen to you Will," she whispered. She picked up the supper plate and tiptoed out of the room, closing the door behind her.

Mattie, her mother, and Jenna were up late that night. They went through the house like the searchers would, to uncover anything that would betray their ties to the Confederate army or the Southern Cause. It amazed Mattie how clever Jenna and her mother had been at disguising things. A barrel of flour with a board on top became an unsuspecting table once covered with a cloth and a lamp. A picture of her father in his uniform was hidden in a frame beneath a baby portrait of herself. The floorboards beneath Jenna's bed would yield an unlikely supply of jam and preserves.

It was midnight as they sat down at the little kitchen table and went over things once again. It was agreed that tomorrow Jenna would go over to the Adamses and ask if Tom could help with the stock. She and Mattie would also milk the cows. That would mean a daily trip to the stockpen. When they were satisfied that the best had been done to secure their possessions, they went to bed.

Mattie slept very little. Thoughts invaded her dreams, images of Will being dragged away, his wound bleeding. Other visions of her father being pushed and shoved away from his family by faceless men in blue uniforms made her wake with a start. Finally, she drifted off to sleep, and was relieved when the daylight woke her. It was Sunday morning.

CHAPTER THIRTEEN

Mattie dressed in her favorite day dress, a blue Zouave with black trim. It had always been her favorite, but now it reminded her of Will, making it extra special. They had decided to hitch the horse and drive into Newtown to church. Will would stay here with Jenna. It was a difficult decision to make, leaving the farm, but after discussing it, Moira decided if they went to church they may hear some news of the army, and find out if there were Yankees in Newtown.

Mattie carried Will's breakfast upstairs, knocking on the door gently.

"Come in, I'm awake," he called.

"Good morning," greeted Mattie as she came over and sat beside the bed, resting the tray on the washstand. He looked tired, and a little pale after the ordeal of the day before.

Will took the musket and leaned it against the wall beside the bed, adjusting his position so he could sit up.

"I hope the Yankees don't come now. By the looks of what Jenna sent me, they'll never believe ya'll don't have any food in this house," he managed a smile, and started eagerly on the eggs and sausage.

"We're going to church. Jenna will be here until we return, then she's going to the Adamses to see if Tom can help with the livestock until we can bring them home."

"I hope so. I'll be alright. I feel much better today and the bandage is only slightly stained, so the bleeding must have stopped."

Later, Mattie and her mother drove to church. It was a beautiful day for the end of August. Sunny, and as if to assert itself that summer should be waning there was a hint of autumn in the crisp air. Life would be perfect if it weren't for the nagging reminders of war.

It had been several weeks since Mattie had been off the farm. Now as they drove down the Valley Pike, they saw the results of an enemy presence in the countryside. Blackened ruins where a barn or house once stood. Barnyards empty of the animal life they had sustained. The road rutted from the hundreds of wagon wheels and pitted by thousands of hooves and boots.

At church they sat in their ususal pew with the Dawsons. Newtown seemed free of Federal troops, but everyone was cautious and the few soldiers in gray who sat near the rear could be seen glancing out the open windows, watching the street, like birds of prey perched for action.

The latest news was of some adventurous exploits of Colonel Mosby. The Rangers had been through Newtown yesterday, and alerted the town of Yankees up at Berryville and north of Winchester. They had raided the Yankee wagon train, and had them so frightened they moved cautiously forward. It would take them a long time to get this far, if indeed they ever found the nerve. Thanks to Mosby and his brave band like Robin Hood of old, many homes had been spared from Hunter's men. Maybe Sheridan's men would be unsuccessful as well.

When Mattie and her mother got home, she went upstairs to see Will, taking the volumn of *Ivanhoe*. It would be good to spend the afternoon reading, keeping their jittery nerves steady. However, the story was so similar to their own circumstances, it only seemed to heighten the tension—Ivanhoe wounded in the side at the tournament, and Rowena and her Saxon escorts taken prisoner, and the gentle nursing of Rebecca. The passages referring to the latter were too close to home for comfort, and Mattie's voice quivered as she read:

> The youngest reader of romances and romantic ballads must recollect how often the females were initiated into the mysteries of surgery, and how frequently the gallant knight submitted the wounds of his person to her cure whose eyes had yet more deeply penetrated his heart.

The discomfort at this sudden baring of her own thoughts made her blush and her throat went dry. She gave a nervous cough.

"I think I need some water." Mattie stopped and averted her eyes from meeting Will's, feeling his stare. She had a pitcher of water and a glass on the washstand for the purpose of refreshment from reading for long periods of time. After drinking until she felt like a camel, she continued:

> In finding herself once more by the side of Ivanhoe, Rebecca was astonished at the keen sensation of pleasure which she experienced, even at a time when all around them both was danger, if

not despair. As she felt his pulse, and inquired after his health, there was a softness in her touch and in her accents, implying a kinder interest than she would herself have been pleased to have voluntarily expressed.

Her voice slowed as she spoke the words, and slowly she brought her eyes up to Will's face. He was looking down at his hands folded on his lap. His face, recently so pale, had flushed, and his cheeks must have felt as hot to him as Mattie's felt. He had a mischievious smile on his face, and cast her a sideways glance, meeting her eyes and raising his brows in an unspoken acknowledgement of what was implied. It was the first gesture of a flirt that she had ever experienced, and it made Mattie tingle all over.

The rest of the afternoon passed without further thought of Yankees. When Mattie read of Ivanhoe's recovery in eight days, it broke the awkwardness and made them laugh, wishing they had some of that medicine for Will. Mattie continued reading until late afternoon. The gallant knight returned to the more comfortable action of battle:

> The love of battle is the food upon which we live—the dust of the melee is the breath of our nostrils. We live not—we wish not to live—longer than while we are victorious and renowned. Such maiden are the laws of chivalry to which we are sworn, and to which we offer all that we hold dear.

CHAPTER FOURTEEN

The next morning found everyone still expectant and on guard. Mattie had been so caught up in the events of the last few weeks, time had passed her by. It was when she was going through her dresses, to see which ones she could rework for something new, that she realized her birthday was one week away. She would turn sixteen on August 22. In the three tumultuous years of the war, she had undergone the transition from child to young lady. Her mother had noticed, and it saddened Moira that these special years, when Mattie should have been enjoying school, picnics, parties, and the carefree days of summer afternoons with friends and family were instead spent on a battlefield, surrounded by death and destruction. She remembered her own childhood, her own sixteenth birthday and she was determined to do something special for Mattie. She had secretly been working on a new blouse for her, and Mrs. Dawson had picked out a new bonnet. On Sunday when they were at church she had given it to Moira without Mattie's knowing.

Will would spend the next two days in bed, and everyone was beginning to relax the vigil, feeling there was no longer any of Sheridan's men nearby. For two days they had seen smoke to the north, above Winchester, and hoped the burning would be confined there.

Moira was at the well, back of the house, when they came. Three dusty men in blue uniforms mounted on rangy horses. They rode leisurely off the Valley Pike and headed toward the MacDonald farm at a trot. It was midday and they were hungry. These Rebels owed them a good meal, that Mosby and his bushwhackers had strung their nerves as taut as bowstrings the last few days. This farm looked quiet enough.

Dismounting in front of the house, they led the horses around to the back, where they could be watered and the saddle girths loosened. Moira was preoccupied thinking about Mattie's party on Saturday, and when she turned from the well with the bucket of water, she looked directly at the three men staring at her. She was so startled that she dropped the bucket of water, and upon realizing they wore Union blue, her heart bounded in her chest.

"What do you want?" she asked, trying to keep her voice steady, her mind searching to remember if there was anything she had neglected to hide. Jenna was in the kitchen, and when she came to the door and saw the men, she gasped and ran back inside.

The leader was stocky and wore an unkempt dark beard. Beneath the dust on the uniform sleeve, Moira could pick out the stripes of a sergeant.

"We're kind of hungry, and since it's dinnertime, decided to share it with you," a gruff voice answered cynically. The other two, younger and lanky, snickered. He seemed like a hard man, but as long as he was halfway civil and all they wanted was something to eat, she would gladly feed them and get them on their way.

"Jenna!" she called. "Jenna, would you fix these men something to eat?"

Jenna peeked from behind the kitchen door. "Yes, ma'am," she said, and Moira could hear the nervous bustling of plates and silverware clinking together as Jenna responded. The men were beginning to look around with curiosity and Moira feared they may get too curious and start snooping. She had to try to keep them out of the house.

"Who else is here with you?" asked the burly sergeant.

"Just the servants and my daughter." She wanted to make it sound like there were more than just three women here all alone, and she didn't want them to know about Will. She picked up the bucket and started drawing more water to replace what was spilled, trying to be casual about it. The soldiers had taken their horses over to the trough and were watering them. Maybe that would keep them busy while she thought what to do.

Meanwhile, Will had heard voices through the window, as all the action was taking place down below his room. He pulled himself out of bed, still in his nightshirt and barefooted. He was surprised how weak he was, all his strength drained away with his blood. He cautiously leaned against the wall and watched the men, out of sight in case they glanced up at the window.

Mattie had heard the horses snorting and come to stand in the hall at the back door. She knew she had to help her mother and together they must use their wits to keep the Yankees out of the house. She didn't like the looks of them, they seemed sullen and not too friendly. Once she felt she had a grip on her fear and her racing heart, she went out to the well where her mother had once again brought up a bucket of water. The men had heard the door and looked over their shoulders at Mattie.

"Can I help you, Mother," she said as calmly as possible.

"Yes, why don't you take some fresh water to the washbasins in the bedrooms." Moira passed the hint to Mattie that she should go up and warn Will. Mattie understood the message.

"Yes, ma'am," she met her mother's eyes, passing unspoken thoughts between them, and taking the bucket, walked towards the back porch.

"Aren't you going to invite us in?" asked one of the troopers. The other two laughed at his rude remark. "Where's that Southern hospitality I've heard about?"

Mattie ignored the remark and kept walking.

"I think I want a house tour," said the sergeant, and they started to follow Mattie.

"Please, we don't want any trouble. I'll gladly give you dinner, but then I want you to leave." Moira tried to assert herself. After all, it was her property. They had no right to just invite themselves in.

But the men ignored the protest, and walked right into the hallway.

Moira was terror stricken, but there was nothing she could do but follow. Once inside the house, Mattie stopped. She couldn't just walk up the stairs, they would probably follow her. The men walked on past her and spread out, each going into a downstairs room. They acted unconcerned, as if they lived there. Moira and Mattie watched as they fingered belongings, turned up cushions, looked at every article and every picture on the wall.

"If you would tell me what you are looking for maybe I could help you," Moira said, her Irish voice sharp with impatience and disgust at this invasion of privacy.

"I think you know what we're looking for," said the sergeant. "More than likely, you've got a husband in the Rebel army. We're just looking for evidence that this house harbors a traitor to the United States." He continued to pilfer.

Moira was dumbstruck. She had heard about it from the other people in Newtown who had been victims of this disgusting practice, but she never realized how horrible and insulting it was to endure.

They finally completed the downstairs search. Then they all three returned to the hallway. The sergeant cast an eye up the stairs.

"Didn't you say you were taking that water upstairs?" He spoke directly at Mattie, looking her in the eye to detect any suspicious behavior.

Mattie had set the bucket down in the hall, it was heavy. Now her heart was in her throat, but she tried to be brave. She looked at her mother, then back at the sergeant, but remained silent. Thinking quickly, she said, "It's only for the bedrooms, I don't have to take it up just now."

"Is anybody up there?" asked the sergeant.

Mattie could not speak. She only shook her head slightly to signify no, hoping the lie was believable.

Whether he believed her or something about her reaction made him doubt, Mattie couldn't tell, but he started up the stairs anyway, followed by the two troopers. She picked up the bucket and, struggling past them on the steps, reached the top before them. She stopped in front of the guest room door, which was slightly ajar, and prayed that they would look in the other rooms first. She went in, expecting to look directly at Will. But the bed was empty!

Where had he gone? She had no time to ponder that, for one of the men followed her inside. She sat the bucket of water by the washstand, her eyes darting around the room for evidence of Will. Suddenly she saw the Zouave jacket draped over the chair by the armoire.

"Why is the bed unmade?" asked the soldier upon seeing the covers disarrayed. He gave her a warning look.

"I was just changing the linens, and hadn't finished." Mattie had moved over by the chair, cautiously, so as not to call attention to what she was doing. The Yankee didn't appear to notice, he was too busy looking under the bed. She threw the jacket on the floor and pushed it under her skirts with her feet, holding it between her shoes. It was well hidden beneath the large hoop. But where was Will? In another bedroom? She held her breath, expecting any moment to hear one of them call out that he had been found.

The men didn't search the upstairs as thoroughly, and finally went back down, satisfied that there were no Rebels here. Mattie kicked Will's jacket under the bed, where the soldier had already searched, and followed him back downstairs.

Will had seen them head toward the back porch. He knew he had to get out of there. It had taken a lot of strength to pull himself out of bed, and even more to climb out the window and onto the roof. There he crouched against the wall, his loaded musket pointed at the window. If a Yankee stuck his head out, Will would blow it off. His breath came in gasps, as a man whose back is to the wall, the pressure of suspense in his chest denying a deep breath. The tin roof was hot on his barefeet. He heard the Yankee in the room, then Mattie's voice, knowing she must be astounded at his disappearance.

Next he heard them on the porch below, their heavy cavalry boots thumping on the steps, and he quickly crawled back through the window, careful not to bang the musket and make any sound. He leaned against the wall once inside, and watched the unsuspecting Yankees as they ate the food Jenna had prepared. They didn't tarry, and soon were back on their horses and heading toward the Valley Pike.

CHAPTER FIFTEEN

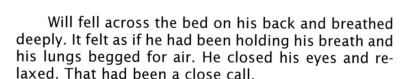

Will fell across the bed on his back and breathed deeply. It felt as if he had been holding his breath and his lungs begged for air. He closed his eyes and relaxed. That had been a close call.

He heard footsteps hurrying upstairs. The door flew open and Mattie and her mother stood with a look of surprise on their faces.

"Will!" Moira said with relief. "Where on earth did you go?" Mattie couldn't figure it out.

He sat up on the side of the bed. "I was out on the roof. I heard you and the Yankee in here." Tension became replaced with nervous laughter. Mattie dragged the Zouave jacket from under the bed and related how terrified she was that the soldier would find it. They were all glad the situation had ended without incident and they could laugh. But it served as a reminder of the type of treatment they could expect from any more enemy intruders.

Mattie suddenly thought about Captain DeCourcey's flag. The Yankees had searched her room and she had forgotten to remove it from the bureau drawer. She jumped up and made a beeline for her room, much to the astonishment of Will and her mother. The drawers were partly open, signifying that they had been ransacked. She bit her lip, and opened the top drawer slowly. The embroidery and needlework were still on top, undisturbed. Burrowing down, she pulled out the little flag, safely hidden between two linen handkerchiefs. It had not been found. She tucked it back underneath, and went back to Will's room, where he and her mother were talking of the farm and the work that would somehow have to be done.

"Where did you go, Mattie?" asked Moira.

"Oh, just to see if those Yankees felt a need to take a Rebel girl's petticoats." They all laughed again.

August 22 came and Mattie turned sixteen. Jenna baked a cake, and they all enjoyed seeing the new blouse and bonnet that she received as a gift from her mother. It was a much simpler celebration than it ordinarily would have been, and Mattie was sorry her father was not there. But these were extraordinary times, and she was pleased just to have a cake. She also knew that without the current circumstances, Will would not be there either, and his presence made it bearable. Once again his side had healed and they resumed reading *Ivanhoe* together in the parlor by day, and singing songs in the evenings. Mattie kept thinking of the day they had read of Rebecca's feelings while nursing the wounded knight, and how Will had flirted. She had liked that and hoped he would continue such signals. But in the days since, he had shown no signs other than as a friend. If this was typical for the way boys acted, she felt she would never be able to tell for sure how he felt. She hoped he liked her, for she had grown fonder of him everyday, and he looked more and more handsome as he regained his health.

The August days passed and September brought occasional cool, crisp ones. Will continued working around the farm, conditioning himself and keeping fit. The apples were ripe for harvesting, and together they spent hours in the orchard, or in the fields threshing wheat and preparing for the winter. Moira kept the cows at the stockpen, still cautious after the affair with the Yankee cavalrymen, and not wanting to risk another of their visits being more fruitful.

One cold rainy evening, they were all in the parlor. Will had built a fire against the damp chill, and the rain pelted the tin roof of the porch outside, covering the sounds of horses in the yard.

Mattie sewed on a shirt she was making for Will while Moira reworked one of her dresses. Will read the newspaper brought over by Mrs. Adams. He was quiet, concerned upon reading about the fall of Atlanta to Sherman's army, knowing it would have grave consequences for the South. All was cozy and quiet, when they were interrupted by a knock at the door. It was so unexpected, Moira didn't move for a moment, but looked at Mattie and Will. They had obviously heard it too, as their eyes met hers, Will's darting cautiously toward the window and the hall. The knock came again. Moira motioned for Will to go upstairs before she answered the door. He quickly was out of sight, and she nervously walked toward the door, bracing herself for another set of intruders.

On the porch stood two rain-soaked figures, water dripping off their hats, which were pulled low over their faces.

"We'd like to come in ma'am and warm by the fire for a little while," said one.

Knowing it would do no good to deny them entry, Moira nodded and stepped aside.

They wore slouch hats, dripping water, and gum blankets, draped around their shoulders, covered their uniforms. Walking casually into the parlor, they came to stand by the fire, quietly facing the heat.

Mattie studied them thoroughly as they had their backs to her, while her mother sat back down and eyed them cautiously. They were tall, and below the blankets Mattie could discern the cavalry boots by the spurs. They did not look around the room, but seemed to sense they were intruders, and wished to be as little bother as possible. They asked neither for food nor drink. Although their hats were pulled down over their eyes, Mattie could see that both were clean-shaven with good features. The blankets hiding their uniforms added an air of mystery to their identity and the purpose of their visit. They talked only to each other in low tones, and did not speak to Mattie or Moira.

The apprehension was getting unbearable, when Mattie saw one of them raise his arm and remove his hat, shaking the water off. Then he put it back on and pulled it down. In that second of raising his arm, the blanket edge fell back to reveal the unmistakable gray cuff of a Confederate uniform. Mattie hesitated to be sure, then asked, "What regiment are you with?"

One man looked at the other, hesitating to answer.

Moira was appalled. What was the girl thinking? Breaking the silence may invite some interrogation that she would rather not have to parry.

After a moment of looking at each other in silent consultation, one of the men spoke.

"Forty-third, ma'am." That was all. The 43rd what? Mattie pondered. Then putting the facts together, she realized who they were. The 43rd Virginia Cavalry— Mosby's men! She looked at them again, just as Moira realized the same truth.

"It's best we don't say too much, that way you can honestly answer any question you may be asked by the Federals as to who may have stopped by here tonight."

The men knew how much families had suffered who had given any aid to Mosby's men. In Sheridan's eyes it was tantamount to treason. Their brief visit to escape the cold rain and warm themselves could cause anguish for this woman and her daughter.

"My husband's with the 33rd," whispered Moira as she continued to sew slowly. "Can you tell us anything about the army?" Her voice had a pleading tone of worry, needing reassurance.

The soldier who seemed to be the spokesman turned to face her. "We rode through Early's lines yesterday. I can tell you that Sheridan is north of Winchester in trenches with Early facing him. Looks like they'll be there for awhile. Neither wants to attack."

The other soldier pulled a gold watch from his vest pocket, then turned and touched the soldier's arm. "It's time," he said.

"Much obliged for letting us stand here and dry off. Evening to you." They nodded and touched their hats, walking into the hall. Moira followed them, watching as they strode off the porch and out into the cold September rain. She heard the jingling of bits and sloshing of hooves in the mud as they mounted and trotted toward the pike.

CHAPTER SIXTEEN

For the next two weeks, the armies faced each other in a game of cat and mouse. As long as Early was between them and Sheridan, the people of Newtown felt safe. Moira still kept the cows away, and Will regained his strength, able to take short walks. Mattie accompanied him, and they would talk of his family and home in New Orleans. He told her of the French Quarter, where the buildings were old and looked like the pictures of Europe she had seen. It sounded so exotic, and reminded Mattie of how she and Captain DeCourcey used to talk. She thought of him, and her father, and knew they were both among the men a few miles away keeping the Yankee army at bay. Will also talked of the other men in his regiment, his Cajun friends, the brothers Jean and Francois, and his best friend whom he referred to as Dee. She sensed that he was anxious to rejoin them.

Moira had noticed the two together. She liked Will a lot, and felt he was a fine young man. At first hesitant

to let them go about together without an escort, she
finally faced the fact that these were far from normal
times. Besides, she trusted Will. After caring for him
these two months, she thought of him as a son. What
concerned her was Mattie's feelings. She knew her
daughter was more than a little fond of him. He was
almost well enough to leave, and most likely would do
so very soon, before his regiment left the area. She
only hoped Mattie had considered that fact.

Now she came into the parlor. It was another one
of those typical fall days in Virginia, brisk and bright,
the sky a deep azure, and the leaves beginning to
turn to the reds and yellows peculiar to maples, and
poplar and dogwood.

Mattie was sewing buttons on the extra shirt she
had made Will. He sat with Andrew's old guitar, picking out the chords to "Lorena."

"It's a lovely day for a walk," she suggested. "Why
don't you two go and tend the cows."

They looked up. Will had become more and more
restless since his recovery, and was eager to keep
busy. He had begun to take on more responsibility
around the farm, splitting and hauling wood, and drawing water for the various necessities of cooking and
cleaning.

"That sounds good to me," he said. "Then maybe
I'll cut and stack some more wood." He put the guitar
back in its corner, while Mattie put away the sewing.
Soon they were off across the fields to the creek where
the cows were hidden, Will carrying a pail for milking.

For awhile, they talked of trivial things, the
weather, the leaves. Once a red fox ran across the
field in front of them and they watched it dart through
the grass with the grace of a cat.

Upon reaching the stockpen, Will turned the cows
out to graze, leaving the pail beside the gate. After a

little while, he would round them up again and milk them. He and Mattie wandered leisurely along the creek bank, leaves drifting down each time the wind rustled the trees. The shady woods were dappled with sunlight, and the cold clear water flowed over rocks in miniature waterfalls, carrying the leaves with the current, like little ships. The banks were steep, and the creek being narrow, they crossed back and forth to the other bank where it was easier to walk.

Mattie followed along behind Will, trying to keep up. With his long strides he had no trouble hopping across the water when necessary. She, on the other hand, had to hold her skirts up with one hand, and try to find rocks on which to pick her way across, using them as stepping stones. Finally the bank became too steep, and teetering on a rock, she lost her balance. "Will!" she called.

He turned to see her trying to perch on the narrow rock, the cold water racing over her boots. Will stepped down the bank and opened his arms.

"Jump!" he called. "I'll catch you."

Mattie leaped toward the bank, almost missing it, and landed with his arms around her waist. She grabbed his shoulders for support, and suddenly, putting one arm behind her knees, he swept her off her feet and carried her up the bank. It was so unexpected, Mattie squealed, then afraid he would fall with her, held tighter to his neck. He started to run with her once on top of the bank, feeling frisky.

"Will! Stop!" she giggled, shutting her eyes tight. "You shouldn't be doing this, what about your side!" She laughed.

He was tiring, even though she was light, and stopped at a large rock. Setting her on her feet, he took her hand and led her toward the rock, where he sat down with his back against it. Mattie plopped down beside him, breathless. They both laughed as they caught their breath.

"Whew!" sighed Will. "I'm not as fit as I thought I was."

They leaned against the rock and rested, still holding hands.

Mattie's head was spinning with ecstasy. Why had he done such an impulsive thing? Whatever the reason, she loved it. Sitting here with him, holding hands, was like a dream come true. He looked at her and smiled, shyly putting an arm around her shoulders. She nestled against him, words unnecessary.

After a few minutes, Mattie asked, "Will, what is it like to be in a battle?" She watched his face for the answer as his gentle expression turned grave.

Will looked straight ahead, but his eyes were seeing visions that weren't there. He rested his head against the rock. "It's like every emotion you've ever had tries to take hold of you at once. You become excited but scared, anxious to get on with the business, but dreading it. Then when your friends all yell, and charge forward, you're caught up in it, too. You get reckless. But it's like watching yourself from a distance, as if you were a witness, not a participant. Does that make sense?"

He looked at Mattie, searching her eyes for understanding, as she simply gave a comforting look, unable to cross the boundary into that masculine world of combat.

"I never thought a battlefield could be so horrible," he continued. "I never would have dreamed that men could die twisted and turned into so many postures."

His reflective mood made her sad. He seemed to need to talk about it with someone. Once again he turned his gaze straight ahead.

"You know what scares me the most though? It's not dying I'm afraid of. But the thought that if I'm killed I won't be sent back to New Orleans. And I can accept that. But I don't want to be tossed in a ditch and marked unknown. I pray that doesn't happen to me. I think the reason I didn't die at Kernstown was that fear."

His words, confiding a personal wish, made her shiver, and she made a solemn vow that if he were to die, she would do all in her power to find him and attend to his burial. Mattie laid her head against his shoulder, feeling his arm strong and protecting around her.

They sat for a long time together, until the time came to milk the cows. Then together, they herded them up and when finished, started the walk back to the farm, holding hands all the way.

CHAPTER SEVENTEEN

The booming of the guns at dawn woke Will with a start. The unmistakable sound of cannon miles away signified that the waiting for battle was over for Early's men.

Mattie sleepily opened her eyes to what she thought was the sound of distant thunder. But soon enough she realized it was guns. She had heard that sound too often in the past. It was only first light, she seldom got up quite so early, but now she was wide awake. She dressed quickly, combed her hair and put it in a hairnet, washed her face and went into the hall. Her mother met her, and Mattie could see the look of concern on her face for the safety of her father.

Will had risen quickly, dressed and gotten downstairs ahead of them. When they reached the foot of the stairs, he was already outside, listening and looking north. Agitated like a horse left behind when its stable mates have gone, he was anxious to join the fray.

The day passed painfully slow for all of them, the sound of the battle pressing on their nerves and minds until all concentration was futile. Mattie and Moira sewed distractedly while Will paced or tried to play the guitar. Finally he went outside, venting his frustration in chopping wood. He knew it was a desperate struggle, for the noise never ceased all day.

At dusk, the sounds of death and destruction stopped. Then the miserable endurance of waiting and anticipating the outcome began. If Early won, more than likely the Valley would be safe from further destruction. If he lost, that would mean a retreat, probably followed by the Union army in pursuit, and more looting and pillaging.

As they sat in the parlor together after supper, nerves taut, silent with each one's thoughts, they heard someone on the porch. It was fully dark by now. Moira drew up her courage for whatever it may be and went to the door. The visitor had already entered, and she walked into her husband's waiting arms. Andrew MacDonald had come home.

His appearance immediately turned her relief into despondency. She looked into the face of a man who had been pushed almost beyond the limits of endurance. He was sweaty and grimy, his hands and face streaked with powder. His right arm hung limp by his side, tied up with a dirty, blood-stained handkerchief. He stood unsteadily on his feet.

"Andrew, are you alright?" She was glad he was alive, but shocked to see him like this. She put her arm around his left side for support, taking his musket.

"It's only a flesh wound, lass." He held her with his good arm. "If you'll clean it and dress it for me, I'll stay long enough to get a little rest."

Mattie and Will had come into the hallway, and stood looking at Andrew. Will could hardly wait to ask about the fighting, but he held his impatience while he helped get Andrew upstairs.

Moira dressed her husband's wound, cleansing it and packing it while he lay on the bed, not even unbuttoning his uniform. He had not lost much blood, and she was confident that it was not a serious wound. "Andrew, please just stay here," she pleaded. After worrying all day, now that she had him home, her reluctance to let him leave persisted.

"I can't darling," he gently insisted. "The Yankees routed us and any wounded left behind will be picked up as prisoners. We left a lot of boys in Winchester because they were too severely wounded to move. Anyone who can walk is retreating. If I don't get back to the company tonight, I'll likely not be able to join them at all."

She convinced him to lie quietly and rest for awhile, bringing water to wash his face, and at least clean up a little. Will had been waiting and saw his chance.

"Do you know anything of the 8th, Sir?" he questioned anxiously.

"Aren't they in York's brigade?" asked Andrew. Will nodded. "Then they covered the retreat, they were the last off the field. I do know General York was wounded, how seriously I do not know. It was a terrible slaughter, lad. We took a heavy pounding today." The distress was apparent in Andrew's face, and his tired voice betrayed the exhaustion he felt by the day long fight. "The army's retreating to Fisher's Hill," he continued, "back into the old trenches there. My regiment went on, but men are falling out all along the roadside, too exhausted to continue."

Within minutes Andrew lapsed into sleep. They left the room to allow him what rest he could catch.

Moira decided to set up a table with a washbasin and towels on the porch. Will brought several buckets of water, and a lantern while Jenna brought plenty of linens. That way, the men coming by could at least wash their faces and clean up a little with clean water before continuing.

As they started outside, there was already a row of jaded bodies sleeping on the porch and in the yard. From the darkness they could hear the clinking and jingling of equipment and the marching feet of the passing army.

Will was torn between staying and going. His regiment was on the road, now would be the time to join them. But he had just gotten back on his feet again, and the wound was still bandaged. After all, it had been less than two months since he was shot. His devotion to Mattie, and knowing they would be left undefended, held him in check. The alternative was risking the Yankees finding him. He stood at the door for a long time looking into the darkness, searching tired faces for a familiar one.

Mattie and Moira returned to the parlor, leaving him alone with the feelings they were unable to share and the concern for his fellow soldiers, his brothers-in-arms.

Two hours later, Andrew left, with a quick hug and a kiss.

The road passing their farm was full of troops all night, but by morning the uniforms had changed from gray to blue. Sheridan's army streamed in pursuit of the Confederates, who stopped at the mountain called Fisher's Hill, their Gibraltar. The hill rose like a sheltering castle of old, temporarily halting the Union advance. But overwhelming numbers can bring down even the walls of a castle, and as Early's men gave up the hill, and retreated farther south, the bodies of many young men were left lying in the trenches they had fought so hard to hold, and many of her sons would never see Louisiana again.

CHAPTER EIGHTEEN

With the Confederate army's retreat toward Strasburg, the Valley was once again laid open to the invaders. Will went down to stay with the cows, both for their protection as well as his own. Sheridan's men were merciless on the families now unprotected by the fathers and sons, brothers and husbands of those left on the farms. The following weeks were forever remembered as what became known as "The Burning", when so many crops and homes were destroyed. Yankees came often to houses seeking food and water, and the MacDonald's farm was conspicuous, being so close to the pike.

Mattie was careful to be sure none were in sight when she went down to the stockpen, taking food to Will and bringing back milk. Now she walked across the fields, trying not to appear in a hurry, looking over her shoulder as casually as she could.

When she was close to the last line of woods she looked around once again, then ran quickly in to the cowpen. Dandy was tethered by the gate and Will was sitting by the fence, his musket leaning within grasp. His blankets where he slept were nearby. He had seen her coming through the trees, and now rose to meet her. He was getting hungry, and this was his noonday meal she brought with her.

"What's going on today?" He was always anxious, knowing the Union army was all around them now. He took the basket of cornbread, ham, and greens that Jenna had packed, and sat back down on the ground. Mattie sat across from him.

"Only some Yankee troops going up and down the road, mostly wagon trains with escorts before I left. But we could see across the pike, and there are fires burning in both directions." Mattie couldn't hide the fear in her voice. She sat watching him eat, these moments together precious, and in spite of all the danger, she lived for this time. She studied his face, memorizing his features to recall later, the gentle expression, the calm blue eyes. He kept a nervous watch, looking around constantly. Suddenly, he froze and stared, then jumped to his feet, upsetting the plate of food. Cautiously, he ran to the edge of the woods. Mattie was puzzled by what he saw, but followed him, looking in the direction of the house.

They could see the black billowing smoke rising above the trees in the distance, and Will knew. It was Sheridan's men burning the MacDonald's barn. All the rage he felt for the enemy flared up inside him. He was a soldier, he should have prevented this. He felt he had neglected his duty by letting this happen, showing his agitation in the way he kept running his fingers through his black hair, shifting his stance from one foot to another, pacing toward the stockpen, yet unable to keep his eyes from the rising smoke and flames. He felt sick in the pit of his stomach.

"Will! That's our barn!" cried Mattie. It was inconceivable to her why they were burning her father's barn. Why would anyone do this hideous deed? What kind of men could be so destructive? Just because her father was fighting for something he believed in, the family should starve, their animals slaughtered? This was supposed to make the South want to rejoin the Union?

"What are we going to do? What about my mother, Will?" The terror in her voice was contagious, and Will's conflicting emotions crowded in on him—fear, anger, frustration, responsibility. In battle he could vent it by fighting, shooting, yelling, even killing. Now he could do nothing but stand by helplessly and watch. He felt tears run down his cheeks. Mattie sat down on the ground, folding her arms on her knees. She sobbed uncontrollably.

"They probably won't hurt her, Mattie, don't worry." He knelt beside her, wanting to comfort her. He reached an arm around her shoulders, and pulled her to him.

Mattie raised her head, and seeing the tears in Will's eyes, felt the mutual need to hold him. Putting her arms around his neck, they sat together on the ground holding each other close, their fledgling feelings of love drowned by the emotions of despair. She cried against his shoulder until his uniform jacket was wet with tears.

Will could tolerate the inaction of a bystander no longer.

"I'm going back, Mattie, you stay here." He grabbed the Enfield and mounted Dandy. Mattie was too distraught to try to stop him and watched, wiping her tears as he galloped across the fields and into the woods separating the field from the house. She didn't want him to go, but concern for her mother was stronger. Within minutes anxiety overcame her, and she too set out for home, half-running across the tall, grassy, rolling hills.

Will stopped at the first line of woods between the farm and where the cows were. He knew one musket was no match for the number of Yankees who would be there. Tying Dandy so he wouldn't bolt, he crept to the edge of the trees. He was close enough to be in range, and he could see the orange flames through the black smoke as the whole frame of the barn was vividly outlined in the blaze. He counted four men in blue, but knew there could be more.

Taking a chance, he loaded the musket and held it to his shoulder. He could take down a few of them before they realized where the shots were coming from. If luck was on his side maybe he could bluff them into thinking they were being attacked by several men.

He picked his target, a man standing a little ways from the others, and pulled the trigger. The man doubled over and fell forward. He quickly pulled the ramrod and rammed another charge down the barrel. Pointing to the other group of three, now aware that one of their number had been hit, he fired again, hitting one man in the leg. He reloaded again, just as a bullet bored into the tree next to him. He fell prone and fired again, but they had scattered.

Just then, a group of horsemen appeared, riders in gray. They routed the Yankees, and shots rang out. There were about twelve cavalrymen that Will could count, and he held his fire so as not to hit friend instead of foe. He ran back to Dandy and mounted, riding hard for the house.

By now, Mattie had reached the trees which Will had just left. She was out of breath, and her lungs ached. Her heart was in her throat anyway, for she had heard the gunshots. Afraid to go any closer she fell down by the trees, catching her breath.

There was scattered shooting, and she too saw the Confederate cavalry. Even though she was exhausted, she stumbled to her feet and continued to run. By the time she reached the backyard, the shooting was over. Although the barn was too far gone to save, the men were throwing buckets of water around it and on it to keep the fire from spreading to the other buildings.

Suddenly from out of nowhere, a rider galloped into the backyard. Mattie looked up to see a black charger, huge and prancing from the excitement. The rider looked directly at her, his blue eyes steady but like his steed alert with tension.

"Will?" she said, puzzled, for he looked identical to Will, with the exception of a trim black mustache above an attractive mouth. He was dressed in an elegant uniform the likes of which had not been seen since the early days of the war, with a feather in his broad-brimmed hat. He was the epitome of a warrior and the words of Ivanhoe rang in her ears:

> The love of battle is the food upon which we live—the dust of the melee is the breath of our nostrils. Such maiden are the laws of chivalry to which we are sworn, and to which we offer all that we hold dear.

It was a fitting description for this gallant knight.

"Whoa, whoa, boy," his calm voice steadied his horse, and he dismounted in front of her.

CHAPTER NINETEEN

"Captain Adolphus Richards, at your service, ma'am," he bowed. Other men joined him, now that the fire was under control. The barn had been totally consumed and destroyed within minutes.

Mattie was speechless, just staring at his incredible resemblance to Will. She was embarrassed at her inability to respond. One of the Rangers spoke.

"One of 'em got away, Dolly," he said disappointedly.

"Well, that pleases me, now he can go and tell Sheridan what happened to the rest."

Dolly Richards walked to where his men were laying out four dead soldiers in blue. They discussed the fight that had just occurred. Will, seeing Mattie, quickly came over to stand beside her. "Your mother is fine, Mattie, she's on the porch."

He guided her to where Moira sat on the top step of the porch, Jenna standing beside her. Her mother looked haggard and defeated, her red hair mussed, strands sticking out of her pinned up coil, and wisps in her face.

"Mother," Mattie hugged her, and tried to control the tears of relief.

"It's all over now, child," her mother reassured her.

Captain Richards walked to the bottom of the steps.

"I'm sorry we got here too late," he apologized, his hat in his hands.

"Nonsense," Moira shook her head, "you arrived just in time. They were getting ready to burn the house," she said with disbelief, wiping her tears.

"Well, we'll teach them what Colonel Mosby thinks of barn burners," he spoke with conviction.

Mattie continued to glance from him to Will, still dazzled by the resemblance. So this was Dolly Richards! She had heard of him, as many people in the Valley knew Mosby's men. Only twenty years old, his bravery was already legendary. Another horseman galloped up, its rider dismounting and gesturing to one of the other Rangers. He then strode over to where they stood.

"Captain Richards," he saluted. "That wagon train will be coming by any time now."

"Very good, get the men mounted except for one or two to help bury those men," he said, then looked back at Mattie and Moira. "We'll put 'em in the woods so none of their friends will see the graves," he suggested.

Will joined the men, loading the bodies of the four dead men on their horses. Taking shovels, they headed toward the woods behind the farm.

"We will do everything we can to protect you while we are in the vicinity," said Captain Richards, and he once again bowed, adjusted his hat, and caught his horse.

He and the other Rangers prepared to leave, Mattie watching with admiration. They were cocky, yet not conceited, and carried on a banter with each other that belied the deadly seriousness of their profession.

Then, as quickly as they had come, they were gone. The quiet yard, so recently the scene of such intense events, was suddenly eerie. The only sound was the fire crackling in the timbers of the barn. Chickens, scattered by the action, now came cautiously back to the yard, clucking and cocking their heads from this side to that, making sure it was safe to venture forth.

Moira stood up, and smoothed her hair from her face with one hand.

"That's the end of our hay for the winter. Now we'll have to use some of the corn for feed instead of meal."

"What we gon do, Miz Moira?" asked Jenna, her hands on her hips. "Dey's done took mos of the apples, too. What's dem men's thank we gon live on?"

Mattie was amused at Jenna's straight forwardness, as if the Yankees should have been more thoughtful. It was true, they had taken all the peaches and apples still in the orchard. Luckily, some of the crop had been picked and stored beforehand.

"We'll just have to be very cautious that more raids will net them nothing. At least they didn't have time to search and find the hiding places."

By the time the women pulled themselves together, Will and the two Rangers had returned. The men mounted, and Mattie watched as they bade farewell to Will, and turning their horses, tipped their hats as they glanced her way, then galloped to find the rest of their command which no doubt was harassing a Federal wagon train about now. Will leaned the shovel against the smokehouse, and came over to the porch. He sat on the steps below the women.

"I'll get you something to drink, Mr. Will," said Jenna as she headed into the kitchen.

Will looked pensive, not speaking. Moira laid a hand on his shoulder.

"Thank you for helping."

Will shook his head. "All I did was distract them long enough for the Rangers to arrive," he smiled. He had something to tell them, and now was as good a time as any. His mind was made up.

"One of the men told me that the army has pulled back to Strasburg," he paused, looking at the ground to avoid their faces. "I think it's time for me to rejoin the 8th."

Mattie's heart sank. She knew this day would come, but refused to face it. It was October 11. He had only been here two and a half months, but she couldn't remember a time without him.

"I'm healed now, and they need every available man. The trouble is the Yankee army is between here and Early. I've got to find a way through their lines."

Moira knew he was right. She knew it was time for him to go, and had sensed the guilt he felt at being safe here when others were dying.

"I have an idea," she offered, "and I'm sure it will work."

CHAPTER TWENTY

The next day was spent preparing Will to leave. Moira and Jenna brought jars of preserves and a ham out of hiding for him to take back to his regiment. The army was hard pressed to feed its own, and every morsel was precious.

The plan was to have Will pretend to be a typhoid victim who had died in the hospital. By lying still, wrapped in blankets, he would ride in the bed of the farm wagon while Mattie and Moira drove him through the lines. If all went well, they could convince the Union pickets that they only wanted to pass through the lines to take the corpse home to his family. Typhoid was very contagious, and in all probability no one would want to inspect the body. They decided to leave at dusk, using the darkness to conceal the fact that their corpse was not really dead if a curious picket did want to take a closer look.

Will was exceptionally quiet and preoccupied during the day. He folded the shirt Mattie had made and an extra pair of socks and drawers, rolling these in his blanket to wear slung across his shoulder, fastened with a piece of rope under his arm. He had very little to carry, and soon all was ready, only the waiting was left. They ate supper in the dining room, a small celebration to say good-bye.

Mattie had tried to prepare herself for this moment, but it was hard to accept his leaving. Nevertheless, she tried to be cheerful. After supper they sat in the parlor. It would be time to leave soon, and Moira left them alone to say farewell in their own way. Sitting on the sofa next to Will, Mattie fought to keep from saying her feelings. What would happen to him now? Would she ever see him again? It was awkward to find something to say. Will took her hand in his, not knowing what to say either.

"Please be careful," she said tearfully as she looked into his eyes. "I'm going to miss you." Her heart was beating so fast it hurt, as she scanned his face, the gentle eyes, high cheekbones, taking a picture with her mind to call up later.

Will felt a new turmoil in his emotions. This was not the same as when he had said good-bye to his parents. This time he felt a reluctance to leave. He had gone over this moment in his head for days. Now he found it difficult.

"Mattie, I have to tell you something," he began slowly, stroking her hand with his thumb. He studied her sad face, her green eyes brimming with tears.

"I love you." The emotion of the words brought them together in an embrace, and Mattie closed her eyes as she felt a tender kiss on her lips. It was the first time she had been kissed by a boy, and she melted in his arms as he hugged her, their cheeks together warm and flushed. She felt her heart race, a flutter inside.

"I've loved you from the first day I saw you," he whispered.

"I love you too, Will. I'll never forget you." It was such a relief to say what she had held silent inside for so long.

"Please don't be sad," he said in her ear. "I promise I'll be back." He kissed her golden hair, and they leaned apart. There was so little time and so much she wanted to say.

Now her mother came in. The time had come.

"We'd best make haste, Will. I need your help to hitch Dandy." The urgency of the situation took precedence, and soon they were in the shed getting the wagon ready.

Moira had some old blankets and wrapping one around himself, Will lay down in the wagon on his back, as straight as a ramrod. They wrapped the other one over him, shroud-like, and carefully concealed his rifle under the blankets close to his side. He would have to hold his breath and be deathly still if anyone did want to look at him, and he practiced this as they started up the Valley Pike. They agreed not to talk, to avoid any slips that may cause the plan to fail. Mattie and Moira had taken two lanterns, now lighted and hung on either side of the wagon seat. Moira drove Dandy. They were all nervous but determined to keep their composure. The road was quiet just now, a little after dark. The Yankee lines were only about five miles ahead. Mattie's thoughts wandered as they lumbered along. Even Dandy seemed to sense the clandestine nature of their mission, and walked cautiously, unsure why he was being driven at night. The moon was not quite full, and gave off just enough light to make shadows distinguishable. She kept thinking of the soft feel of Will's kiss, and the thrill it had given her. Now he would be gone in a few hours.

She glanced back at the still form beneath the blankets, and it gave her an eerie chill, like a premonition that could come true. She shook it off and turned her mind away from the unpleasant prospect.

"Are you sure this will work, Mother?" she asked doubtfully, afraid of the consequences.

"It has to work, child." Moira sounded determined. "It has to."

Please God keep him safe! I love him too much. She prayed silently.

Will decided to take the opportunity to try and sleep beneath the covers. He would probably be up most of the night trying to find his regiment. As he closed his eyes and tried to relax against the jolting frame of the springless wagon he was thinking of Mattie, and soon he drifted into a light sleep.

"Mother, what do we do if they want to see him?" asked Mattie.

Moira shook her head. "I suppose we'll have to let them look and pray they don't feel the urge to prod him with a bayonet."

The time passed, and the road remained quiet. Finally, they could see the thousands of tiny lights against the fields and rolling hills, like so many stationary fireflies. On either side of the pike, the Union camp seemed to fill the Valley floor.

Moira stopped Dandy, listening for any voices, but they were still too far from the pickets.

"Let me talk to them, Mattie. If they do ask you anything, remember—we're taking him to his family in Strasburg. We must not seem suspicious at all." Moira reached back and shook Will's shoulder, waking him.

"Will, we're just outside the Union camp. Be prepared for anything." She clucked to Dandy and they started forward.

A few yards farther and they approached several Yankee soldiers, standing casually, leaning on their arms, on either side of the road. Their idle chatter ceased as the wagon approached. Moira slowed to a stop as one stepped forward at Dandy's head, another coming alongside her seat.

"Halt!" A sentry's rifle clattered as he came to attention. The man beside Moira held a lantern to her face.

"Yes? What business do you have?" He was a young lieutenant, not older than Will, but seemed as inexperienced at soldiering as his fresh new uniform.

"I am Mrs. Moira MacDonald. I have a man who died, and I am taking his body to his family in Strasburg. I hope you will be so kind as to let us pass."

She kept her voice polite and steady.

The young officer walked to the back of the wagon and looked in, holding his lantern up.

"Private Williams, would you come here?" he called. Another soldier, shouldering a rifle and also carrying a lantern, joined him. Together they glanced at the long still form of the blankets, seeing no movement. Then they began to look on either side of the body, and the sergeant noticed the food in the corner of the wagon bed.

"Why is this food here?" he asked curiously.

Moira's mind was quick. "It's for the funeral, his family are dear friends of mine," she said confidently. The soldiers continued to stand, and Mattie was getting nervous. Will couldn't hold his breath forever.

Meanwhile, Will was doing just that. He had felt them poking around, one move of a muscle could betray him.

The lieutenant reached in unexpectedly, and pulled the blanket off Will's face. He froze, shutting his eyes tight. They held the lantern aloft, bathing his features in its soft light.

"Why did he die?" asked the officer, caught off guard by the sight of one his own age, his own mortality on his thoughts.

"He contracted typhoid. He has been in the hospital in Newtown since being wounded at Winchester."

Moira was shaking, but controlled her voice and hoped it didn't show in the dark.

"He only died this afternoon, that's why we are so late. They didn't want him left at the hospital, since typhoid is so contagious."

The lieutenant covered Will's face quickly and stepped back in a gesture of disgust.

"Very well, you can pass. I will write you a pass to go through our lines. Show it when you're stopped." He and the private left and went over to a table holding a field desk, and placing the lantern on a stand, began to write and sign a piece of paper.

Will was sweating despite the October chill, and his heart was pounding so hard he was afraid the Yankees would hear it. He tried not to breath, but it seemed the more he tried not to, the greater the need.

Mattie was shivering with nerves, and her mother quietly and firmly put a hand on her arm to steady her. They were almost home free.

The lieutenant walked back to her.

"This is all you need. Good evening ma'am," he said and walked away, Moira clucking to Dandy. They had passed the first hurdle and now entered the heart of the enemy camp.

Suddenly the road became busier, men walking up and down the pike to various duties and areas of the camp. Moira and Mattie were awed at the might of this vast army. The hundreds of wagons and ambulances in the transport, the rows of tents shining in the partial light of a dim moon. And scattered within it all, the thousands of fires signifying the number of soldiers sent against their army—against her father, and Will and Captain DeCourcey.

They kept a steady pace and safely passed the last picket post, showing the pass. They had made it. Will breathed a sigh of relief.

CHAPTER TWENTY-ONE

When she was sure they were well outside the Union lines, Moira pulled Dandy up, and turned around.

"Will!" she whispered. "It's safe."

He slowly pulled the blanket off his face and leaned up on one elbow.

"Where are we?" he asked, looking around in the darkness.

"I'm not certain, but about two miles from Strasburg, I think," said Moira.

The Rangers had told Will the army had pulled back to Hupp's Hill below Strasburg. He decided it would be best if he took to the woods and headed toward his lines that way. He had no idea where the 8th was, but if he could just find the Confederate pickets he would be safe. He had to get there while it was dark to avoid detection. Who knew what daylight would bring.

Throwing off the blankets, he hopped out of the wagon and adjusted his equipment. He quickly put the food in a pillow case given him for the purpose and was ready. Mattie and Moira climbed down and walked to where he stood behind the wagon. There was no time for all the things he wanted to say.

"Mrs. MacDonald, I don't know how to thank you—," he began awkwardly.

"Go, son, you must hurry," said Moira as she gave him a motherly hug. "Be careful."

He turned to Mattie, and taking her hand squeezed it, giving her a quick kiss. She could not see his face in the dark, but he whispered, "Remember what I said." Then he backed away, and turning quickly on his heels, was gone.

Mattie watched his figure disappear into the dark mass of trees. She wanted to cry but held her eyes shut tight to keep from it. Her mother put an arm around her shoulders, rubbing her to comfort the hurt she knew her daughter must feel. Mattie leaned her head against her mother's shoulder.

"I love him, Mother," she said, stifling a sob.

"I know you do, dear," Moira was sympathetic. "We'll pray for him." After a moment of silence, they climbed back into the wagon.

"We can't go back just yet. If the same picket is on duty, he'll realize we haven't had time to go to Strasburg. We'll just sit for a little while and wait."

It was a clear night, and cold. They wrapped the lap robe across their knees and used the blankets for wraps around their shoulders. Sitting alongside the road, they could see the dark silhouette of Massanutten Mountain in the distance against the lighter shade of the sky, the stars like a curtain backdrop. Moira thought of her husband somewhere out there beyond them. Mattie now knew three men, dear to her, that the war threatened.

Will could follow his path south by the outline of the mountain and the stars. He knew he had to run into the lines somewhere in this direction. By carefully keeping parallel to the road, but out of sight, he should be there in an hour or so. He walked cautiously, the dead leaves snapping beneath each step. Occasionally he would stop and crouch, listening and searching the darkness as far as he could see. The last thing he wanted to do was walk into a nervous picket post unannounced.

The woods ended and formed the edge of an open field. Will studied it, and decided to cross. The grass felt dry and brittle beneath his feet, and the smell of burnt ground greeted his nose. Once a wheat field, now acres and acres of blackened land stood as a testimony to the merciless nature of Sheridan's army. Across the field a narrow line of woods broke the landscape. Will stopped and cautiously picked his way through. There at the foot of Hupp's Hill he could see the many orange lights of countless campfires marking the Confederate lines. Surely there was a picket post nearby. Approaching cautiously, he listened for voices, and hearing the familiar drawl of Southern accents, called out, "Don't shoot! I'm looking for my regiment!" He crouched quickly as he heard rustling and the cock of rifle hammers.

"Who goes there?" asked a voice.

"Private William Hamilton, 8th Louisiana Infantry!" called Will.

"Come forward!"

Will walked toward the sound, now marked by lanterns. He found himself in the company of two sentries in uniforms that could use some mending. They looked tired and defeated. Uncocking their muskets, they carefully leaned on them. "I'm looking for the 8th Louisiana. Do you know about where they're camped?" asked Will.

"All the Louisiana troops are on the right of the line, in Gordon's Division." The soldier pointed, a tall lean man in his thirties. "You've entered about middle way."

"Thank you for your help. I've been away since Kernstown. I was wounded and stayed with a family about five miles from here," said Will, trying to explain his sudden appearance.

"Well, you're lucky boy, you missed two disastrous battles," said the other soldier, a short man with a blondish beard, chewing tobacco casually. He spit, disgustedly.

"What's the word on the next action?" asked Will. They both frowned and shook their heads.

"Who knows with Early in charge," said the other. Will got the impression these men were not happy with recent events.

"Well, I'll be on my way," and nodding a good evening, they parted.

Will wandered down the line of regiments, asking first here then there. The familiar noises of an army camp greeted him, this group of men around a fire talking, another group singing. Finally he came to his old regiment and found his company.

It was just after midnight when Will strolled into the camp of the Bienville Grays. The campfire was bright, surrounded by several figures talking and a couple of prone bodies wrapped in blankets, sleeping on the ground by the warmth. Will recognized the familiar voices and faces, the peculiar accents of Jean and Pierre. It was like a homecoming of sorts. The bond he had formed with these men was as strong as any marriage. He sauntered toward the firelight, unnoticed at first. Dee Monaghan was rubbing down the stock of his rifle with a cleaning rag, when he glanced up. He stared for a minute afraid his eyes were deceiving him.

"Will Hamilton!" He sprang to his feet. "We thought you were dead!"

He was joined by the two Cajuns. They gave Will hugs, slaps on the back and handshakes sufficient for a reception of one back from the dead.

"What happened to you? I caught sight of you in that charge at Kernstown, then suddenly you just weren't there." Dee had been Will's best friend since joining the 8th. They had vowed to look out for one another every time there was a battle. With his blonde hair and ruddy face, he was just the opposite of Will in appearance.

"I was hit and knocked down." Will pulled his shirt out of his trousers, and raising one side, revealed the bandage. "I knew I couldn't keep up with ya'll so I went to a tree in the woods and passed out."

"I came back to look for you later, but I must have missed you in the dark," Dee smiled. "I'm glad you're alright." He laid a hand on his shoulder as he said it.

"We also lost Francois in that charge," said Jean de Lechard. His grief was still evident in his voice at the loss of his younger brother. How would he tell their mother.

"I'm sorry to hear that Jean," said Will, genuinely saddened. "Things won't be the same around this camp without Francois."

Francois had been the camp clown, always play-ing pranks and being mischievous. He and Jean were the only two who had managed to retain the scarlet skullcaps with the gold tassels which had been part of the original Zouave uniform. Now Jean was the only one.

"I saw it happen," added Pierre. "He was hit by an artillery shell. There was nothing left—"

He shook his head and looked away as if to stop the terrible memory from haunting him. Jean had tears in his eyes, and Will laid a hand on his arm. These were his brothers-in-arms. They had shared many experiences together, good and bad, and friendships like these, forged in war, were strong.

Will stacked his rifle with the others, and hung his equipment over the bayonet points.

"I brought you something," he said, as he opened the pillowcase to reveal the ham, bread, and preserves sent by Moira. His comrades were overwhelmed with gratitude, having had scarcely any meat ration for weeks now. Their winter would be bleak and hungry.

"So, did this family have any pretty daughters?" asked Pierre slyly, changing the subject from one of pain to pleasure. He always was one for the ladies, and was handsome in his French looks, dark and well groomed with a neatly trimmed mustache. The others snickered.

"As a matter of fact, they did," said Will shyly. They could tell he was blushing even in the firelight.

"Oh, and so now Will has a sweetheart," said Jean as he elbowed Will good-naturedly, fingering his jacket and insinuating with a look that he was envious of the coveted uniform.

Will nodded an acknowledgment.

"What's her name, Will?" asked Dee, between bites of ham and biscuit. None of the young men were married and talking about girls was one of their favorite topics.

"Matilda," he said. "Her father's in the 33rd Virginia. So tell me, what's the word on our next move?" Will wanted to change to a more comfortable subject. He felt shy talking about his new role as a sweetheart. The men became more serious.

"The army has lost two battles and many men in less than a month. Our regiment alone is down to half its strength, and our company—"

Jean shrugged and shook his head. "It will cease to exist if we keep on like this." He stared at the fire, eating a piece of the ham that Will had brought.

"Especially without Captain DeCourcey," said Dee as he continued to work on his rifle. "That Lieutenant Pierce who's in charge is just not experienced enough."

Will perked up. "What happened to Captain DeCourcey?" he asked, afraid of the answer.

"He was taken prisoner," said Jean.

Despondent at this latest piece of news, Will hung his head and leaned it into his hands. "Is that for certain?" he asked after a pause, the hopelessness showing on his face.

"Oui, I was there," said Pierre. "It was that shoulder. He had never regained his strength in it. His horse shied at an artillery shell, and jerked the captain's arm. He fell, unable to hold his mount. This was on the retreat from Winchester, it was only a moment before he was surrounded."

They all lapsed into silence at the thought of this loss, and fearful of the consequences for their captain. Knowing the prison conditions in the North, death was as possible there as it was on the battlefield. Perhaps more so.

Once again Will was back as a member of the Bienville Grays, and spent the next hour reminiscing before they all turned in for the night.

CHAPTER TWENTY-TWO

The next week spent in camp with old comrades found Will settled into his former role as soldier, but he discerned an obvious change since he had been away. Morale was low and the lack of shoes and food further debilitated the strength of Early's army. Some, like the sentries that first night back, had lost all confidence in their commander.

The weather was exceptionally beautiful on October 18, a clear crisp fall day. Spirits were high despite the privations in the camp of the Bienville Grays. One of the men had managed to get a letter from his Louisiana home and shared all the news with his fellow soldiers. Apparently, things had calmed down there while Sherman and Grant made the war in the East the center of Union aggression, while General Dick Taylor kept the Yankees busy in East Louisiana.

Will was sitting on the ground, using his knee as a desk, writing a revised letter home. Some mail was getting through, and he wanted desperately to let his mother and father know he was alive. He closed it carefully, folding the paper to create a self-made envelope, and addressed it. Jean and Pierre returned from one of their foraging expeditions, finding nothing to eat. Some of the ham that Will had brought was still left, and Dee was cooking cornbread.

The new lieutenant who had replaced Captain DeCourcey appeared and calling them all to attention, ordered the cooking of two days' rations and to be prepared to march at nightfall. No details were given, and Lieutenant Pierce was a man of few words anyway. But Will and his friends knew the orders meant fighting.

The last hours in camp were solemn as each man prepared himself in his own way for an uncertain fate, and Will's thoughts were on Mattie. It had been a week since he left her, and he wondered if she missed him as much as he did her. He sat by the fire, staring at the glowing coals. Tents were few, and in his company there were only five among the remaining twenty men. Only twenty men left, thought Will. The Bienville Grays had left New Orleans in 1861 with a company of 130 men. Their story was the same as all the other companies of young men whose enthusiasm in the early days had been so contagious.

By 8:00 p.m. the soldiers in Gordon's Division stood ready to march. It was to be a silent all-night march, to surprise the Union left flank, and all canteens and equipment that would clink or jingle were left behind in a pile. Will wore only his uniform, necessary accouterments, and a new slouch hat he had acquired once back in camp. He carried only his rifle and haversack of rations. All lives and the battle plan depended on absolute silence, and the long, gray line picked its way stealthily along a path between the Shenandoah River and Massanutten Mountain, a silent snake crawling toward the Yankee lines to coil for a strike.

Will marched behind Dee, followed in turn by Jean and Pierre. They said nothing, no cheerful banter that usually accompanied a march, and Will was impressed at the cooperation of thousands of men dedicated to the success of victory. The moon lit their single file path in the dark, until they came to Bowman's Ford, where they would cross the river. Here they waded waist deep into the chilly, early morning water. Will shivered as he held his musket above his head, his teeth chattering, and anxious to reach the bank now under a blanket of fog. Once out, they quickened their pace, and soon encountered the startled Yankee pickets. The opening phase of the Battle of Cedar Creek had begun.

CHAPTER TWENTY-THREE

Mattie had been fighting a case of the blues all week. She missed Will terribly, finding herself daydreaming while she sewed, or fed the chickens, distracted by thoughts of him. Closing her eyes she tried to recall his face, each feature, his smile. How she wished he could have had a photograph made of himself to give her before he left.

October 19 dawned foggy. Mattie was up unusually early, and dressed quickly in the early morning chill. Upon reaching the warmth of the kitchen where Jenna had already prepared a crackling fire, she plopped down sleepily in a chair near the heat.

"Good morning," Jenna said cheerily. She had already cooked one pan of biscuits and was making coffee, eggs and bacon. The baking smells and sizzling meat greeted Mattie's nose and she felt comforted by the cozy room.

"It sure smells good, Jenna," she said. "I'm starving."

Jenna was busy rolling more biscuit dough out on the table. "I sho miss Mr. Will," she said. "That boy did love my biscuits. And it was good to have a man around here. It's been hard to look after thangs with dem Yankees stealing it all."

"I know. Mother wants us to bring the cows back today. It's just too much trouble to tend them way down there." Mattie thought of the day she and Will had first held hands and sat by the rock. The memory was peculiarly sad and sweet at the same time. Suddenly in the quiet they heard a booming sound, low and distant. Jenna stopped her work, and Mattie looked at her.

"It's guns," said Mattie, her heart sinking. How many more times would that sound invade her happiness and fill her with fear? She leaped up and threw open the kitchen door, running outside. Standing in the foggy morning mist, she listened. Her mother appeared from the back door, still in her nightgown, her hair in a long braid. They both stood looking south into a curtain of fog. The sound was louder without the thick walls and solid wooden door of the kitchen for a buffer. It came from across the Valley Pike to the southeast, the foot of Massanutten Mountain. The sound reverberated off the mountainsides.

Moira walked down the steps of the porch, her mind fighting the nagging thought that events in progress could have grave consequences. Many lives would never be the same after those guns stopped. Possibly her own.

After the initial thought of Andrew and Will, came the dread of what to prepare for. If the Yankees retreated, they would come back down the Valley by the farm. If the Confederates pursued, her very fields could become a killing ground. Should they pack what they could and leave or sit tight? Her mind debated the choices. It would do no good to go to Mrs. Adams, her farm was even closer to the battle. She decided the best thing to do would be to go into Newtown.

"Mattie, I want you to take whatever you can carry from your room and pack it in your small trunk."

Mattie was distressed by her mother's orders. If they were leaving it must be dangerous. They had stayed through so much else—Hunter, Kernstown and Winchester; the Yankees burning the barn, the ruins of which still lay in its ashes. After all that, they must finally leave their home?

"First, we'll finish breakfast since Jenna has it ready." Moira stood beside her daughter, an arm around Mattie's shoulders. She tried not to sound too alarming. "I think it's best we go into town, we'll visit the Dawsons. It will be safer there."

Mattie was silent. She wanted to stay, to be as near Will as possible. What if he were wounded again? He might come there. Or if he were killed? She remembered her silent vow.

They were too nervous to eat much, the guns continuing to pound, the sound escalating with the passing of time. They packed what they didn't eat, and began gathering clothing and valuables. Mattie opened the lid to the trunk and began folding clothes and linens. She remembered the little pelican flag and once again packed it safely between her embroidery, concealing it in the trunk. Soon, she was ready.

"Please keep them all safe," she prayed for her soldiers.

They hitched Dandy, and Jenna and Moira closed the shutters and secured the house and kitchen as best they could. The livestock was turned loose to fend for itself, except the cows which were left penned up at the creek. Then climbing into the wagon, and bidding a last look back, all three women headed toward Newtown, away from the sound of battle.

CHAPTER TWENTY-FOUR

The Confederate line of Gordon's Division, made up of Georgians, Louisianians, and Virginians, hit the Yankee pickets hard and were met by artillery fire. Will and the other men of the 8th, their fighting blood roused, ran forward with a Rebel yell, and within fifteen minutes had pushed the enemy soldiers back across the Valley Pike.

Now the air of battle engulfed Will. The uneasiness of waiting over, once again engaged in conflict, his nerves became steel as he defied danger. A feeling of being immortal had taken hold just as it does for all soldiers under fire.

He loaded and fired his Enfield with seasoned expertise, occasionally glancing on either side at Jean or Dee, who were caught up in the moment as if at some sporting match. Running through the fog, they pursued the enemy through their own camps. The Union army had been caught unprepared, just beginning to start the day.

As Will and his comrades hit the camps, they were greeted by the smell of ready coffee and frying bacon. His stomach responded, reminding him that they had eaten nothing for almost 24 hours. The march had been non-stop, sleepless, and followed by the superhuman effort of fighting. It was too much of a temptation.

Jean and Pierre, always alert for plunder, dropped their guns and immediately began to partake of the bounty. Will had continued on, until he realized men were stopping left and right of him, as unconcerned as if they were going shopping instead of fighting a battle. He slowed his steps, finally halting and turning back. The charge lost its momentum.

"Dee! Come on!" he called, waving his arm forward. Even Dee had taken advantage of the opportunity to eat. He stood leaning his musket in the crook of his arm, while he ate.

"Oh, come on Will! We licked 'em. They ran!" He grinned broadly.

"Look at all these good things, why waste it?"

Will stood dumbfounded, watching as men ransacked tents, and finding shoes and trousers relatively unused, were actually taking the time to change clothes! The unbelievable wealth of the Union army was there for the taking. Not only food, but men loaded themselves down with everything from cooking utensils to extra blankets. He felt ridiculous not to join in. Perhaps the battle was over. The Yankees had retreated full tilt, why should they come back? He walked back to the campfire where Dee stood, now helping himself to a cup of coffee. He poured one for Will.

Jean and Pierre joined them, as happy as boys on Christmas morning. Incredibly Pierre had found a Zouave jacket belonging to some New York regiment and was wearing it proudly. Jean sported a new overcoat, a much needed article in the coming winter months. Will only hoped they weren't mistaken for the enemy in the fog.

The battle still raged ahead of them, being sustained by those men who had not stopped to plunder. Will felt the call of duty.

"Dee, I'm going on ahead with the regiment," he gulped the rest of the coffee and crammed bacon and bread in his haversack for later.

"Wait for me, I'm coming!" Dee called after him.

Will ran cautiously through the foggy air until he came upon the rear of the Confederate line. The battle turned nasty. Some Yankee regiment was stubbornly fighting back, and the strong push of the Southerners was just as stubborn. Fighting became yards apart, then hand to hand. Will fought with mechanical accuracy, all concentration intensely centered on the business of clubbing and bayoneting blue-clad figures. Then he found himself confronted by two soldiers at once. He had no time to load his gun, so parrying first one, then the other, he stabbed with the bayonet. They were too fast. One hit him in his right side with the butt of a musket, across his old wound. He had not worn a bandage since returning to camp, and the blow, which would have doubled him over anyway, was twice as painful against the still tender flesh.

He tried to recover, and looking up, stared into the eyes of his attacker, who briefly hesitated. A split second of contact between two men trying to kill each other, then Will was aware of the stock of the rifle coming toward the side of his head.

Blinding pain, a feeling of displacement from his physical body, and reeling backward he fell. Darkness and dizziness engulfed him, the sounds around him died away, and he faded into unconsciousness.

Will awoke slowly with a searing pain which throbbed through his head with every beat of his heart.

He was aware of someone groaning, and was annoyed, wishing whoever it was would be quiet. Then as he became conscious, he realized it was himself who was making the sound. He gained control of his voice, and lying still put a hand to his aching head. He felt blood, and a knot which smarted at the lightest touch. He was flat on his back, his body so exhausted and racked with pain, he felt no inclination to rise.

He became aware of the immediate area around him, and saw bodies lying all about, some clad in blue, some in gray, huddled in the grass. There was no sound of shooting. All seemed calm, and the fog had given way to the warm October sun, the feel of it on his face giving back some sense of life. Turning his head, he saw a familiar blonde head a little ways off. It was Dee Monaghan, wisps of his hair moving in the gentle breeze. But he did not move. Slowly and in agony, Will crawled to his side.

"Dee," he tried to call, but his voice was weak. Grabbing his jacket at the shoulder, he pulled him over. The lifeless body of his friend was limp and unresponsive. Will felt his spirit sink inside. He wanted to die himself. His best friend was dead and his own body fought a tormenting pain. He sank back in the grass, his strength drained.

Soon familiar voices greeted his ears, the French accents were unmistakable. Jean and Pierre were searching among the dead and wounded for their friends.

Will summoned his strength. "Here! Jean!" he called. His throat was as dry as cotton. They had heard, and finding Will, gently raised his head, Pierre giving him a drink from his canteen. Then they gently helped him sit up.

"Are you wounded?" asked Jean. Will shook his head.

"Just took a butt stroke in my side and a blow to the head. But Dee—" His voice cracked as he pointed to their friend.

Will leaned on Jean, slowly getting up, as Pierre kneeled beside Dee's body, gently cradling his head on his lap. Suppressing anger, he fought tears, until he lost the battle and they ran down his cheeks. He searched Dee's clothing for his personal effects to send the boy's mother. If they left him here he would more than likely be robbed. They would return later and bury him.

The lull in the battle which gave time for these events lasted long enough for Will to return to the Yankee campsite, still a source of plunder. Here he rested and recovered, until late that afternoon, when the Yankees unexpectedly counterattacked. Will stumbled along on a retreat back to Fisher's Hill in the darkness. The brilliant victory of the morning had turned into a loss by nightfall.

CHAPTER TWENTY-FIVE

Mattie sat in the front parlor of the Dawson's house with Emmaline. The guns had ceased shortly after noon, and she was too restless to do much of anything. The war had totally disrupted any schooling she would ordinarily be getting. In fact, all of the schools had been closed. Her mother had encouraged her to return to her studies since Will left, and now she and Emmaline worked on their French together. But who could concentrate on studying French with a war going on! Mattie thought the idea absurd. "It will keep your mind occupied," her mother had said.

Well, it wasn't working. The guns had been silent now for two hours, and Mattie wanted to go home. There had been much Union traffic through Newtown, first all the transports retreating from the battle front, which the MacDonalds had arrived just ahead of, then suddenly forces rushing through town towards the battle. It was confusing to try to ascertain what was happening. It was even reported that General Sheridan himself had ridden through at a gallop on his way from

Winchester toward the action. All the rumors and speculation simply made her more restless. Only Will filled her thoughts.

"Emmaline, I simply can't think anymore!" said Mattie as she slammed the French book shut.

Emmaline closed her's too. "I know, I don't blame you. If my sweetheart were at the front, well, I just don't know what I would do." Emmaline never seemed to know what she would do about anything. It was little comfort to her friend.

Mattie's mind wandered. "I hope he's alright," she thought out loud, leaning on her elbows and staring out the window onto the main street.

Emmaline followed her gaze. "Do you think he will write you letters? I think it would be so romantic to get a letter from a soldier." She dreamily looked out the window at the street, quiet for the moment.

"I suppose he will, as soon as things settle down. Maybe he'll even come back to the farm, especially if we win the battle!" Mattie's hopes rose.

Moira came in. "Mattie, somehow I don't believe you are concentrating on your French. And don't lean on your elbows, it isn't ladylike."

"Yes, ma'am," said Mattie putting her arms down. "Mother, when can we go home?"

"Mrs. Dawson has invited us to stay the night and I feel that is best." She smiled sympathetically at her daughter. "Maybe we'll hear some news if we stay in town. Hopefully we can leave in the morning." Knowing nothing she could say would really help, she left again.

Mattie pouted, opening her French book and staring blankly at the page.

"Mattie, did Will ever kiss you?" Emmaline was curious about subjects she herself had no experience in.

Mattie smiled shyly, and nodded. "Once," she looked at Emmaline.

"What was it like?" asked her friend in awe, giving Mattie a feeling of superiority.

She thought for a moment. How could she explain such a wonderful feeling?

"It was very quick, I didn't have much time to think about it really. But it was nice." She blushed, surprised at her embarrassment in front of Emmaline.

That afternoon passed, the guns resuming their nerve-racking booming. After supper, the Dawsons sat in the parlor, joined by Mattie and Moira. Mr. Dawson was at a town meeting and they waited anxiously for news of the fighting.

By 9:00 p.m. Mr. Dawson had returned. As he walked into the parlor, all eyes were riveted on his face. The gravity of the situation showed in his expression. He stood in the middle of the room as if to make an announcement. Only the ticking of the clock on the mantel disturbed the silence.

"The battle ended just after dusk. General Early has retreated to Fisher's Hill, and Sheridan is now in control of the whole lower Valley." He slowly took off his hat, and sank heavily into a chair beside the fire, distractedly reaching for the poker and turning the wood.

"Oh, no," groaned Moira, leaning her head into her hands. Mattie felt her own heart sink.

"There were two Union officers standing on the street corner as I passed on my way home. They were elated. Said there was going to be much celebrating in their camp tonight." He related the incident with disgust.

They were all solemn, and went to bed early to sooth the hurt with sleep. Mattie cried in her pillow, and prayed that none of their loved ones had become a casualty that day. The next morning she, her mother and Jenna started for home, bracing themselves for whatever may greet them. Upon reaching the farm, everything was just as they had left it. The battle tide had not reached that far.

CHAPTER TWENTY-SIX

The next few weeks saw the Union army completely pull out of the Shenandoah. The Confederate Army of the Valley had ceased to exist. All elements of Early's command were dispersed to other parts of the state, most to the siege lines at Petersburg. For the first time in almost four years, there was peace in the Shenandoah.

Will and the remnants of the 8th were among those sent to the Petersburg lines. Cedar Creek had taken an irreparable toll on the Louisiana regiments, making them almost unfit for service. They had hoped to be furloughed home but instead found themselves in a deplorable condition of trench warfare. Scanty rations, low morale and the winter cold further depleted the Bienville Grays. Now there were only 10 of them left. Jean, Pierre, and Will had survived thus far and Will had managed to get a letter home to his parents and receive one in return. They had been worried and were relieved to learn that their only son was still alive.

Will fought the March chill and wind to write a letter to Mattie. Although the army had remained at Fisher's Hill for weeks after the battle, he had been unable to visit because of the Yankee army still in the area. Then January and February brought the most severe winter weather in ten years. Shelled continually by the ever growing and well-fed enemy, and starving, the Louisianians were once again called on to spearhead the breakout and end the stalemate. After an action at Fort Stedman, they formed the rear guard as Gen. Robert E. Lee led his small force to a Virginia town called Appomattox. There on a Palm Sunday morning in April he surrendered the Army of Northern Virginia.

For Mattie, life was approaching the closest thing to normalcy she had experienced in almost four years. The most significant difference was the shortage of food for both man and beast, since most crops had been destroyed during the fall harvest. Money ceased to buy the barest necessities, and they lived sparingly. At least the sounds of war were gone. With Palm Sunday behind them and Easter coming, they could begin a renewal of the spirit with the spring. Now she sat in the parlor, fingers trembling as she opened a letter from Will. Mrs. Adams had just brought it, as she had gone into Newtown to find a few meager supplies. The letter was dated March 12, a month ago, and had arrived by way of a returning soldier furloughed home with a wound. A member of the 33rd Virginia, who Will had sought out to send the letter, also brought one from Andrew MacDonald. It was some relief just to see his handwriting, signifying that at least he was still alive just a month ago. Unfolding the mud-stained paper, she read:

My Dearest Matilda,

    I managed to obtain piece of paper and am writing to let you know all is well with me here. This part of the line has been quiet of late, and we are glad to see the weather beginning to warm. Our thin blankets were a poor cover against the chill of February. We are only fed every other day now, and I don't see how we can hold out much longer. Some of the men are feeling very despondent and desperate. Jean did a very reckless thing with the Yankee pickets last week. While he was on picket he hollered over at the Yankee counterparts. Our trenches are very close together here and we often yell back and forth to each other. This particular Yank knew we were on short rations and told Jean if he waited until dark he could come over and they would give us some meat. We tried to talk him out of it, but he went anyway. About an hour later he returned with all sorts of good things to eat. I guess they felt sorry for us. You should see me, I've lost weight. Be sure and tell Jenna I would love some of her biscuits now. I will try to write more later. I miss you more each day and can hardly believe it has been almost five months since we parted. Tell your mother hello from me.

With affection,

    Your Will

    Mattie thought no one could possibly know how wonderful it feels to find out a loved one is safe until they've experienced the terrible waiting and wondering. She hugged the letter to her, and after reading it a half dozen times more, took it up to her room. Carefully putting it away in the drawer where Captain James's flag still lay, she sat down and began to write a letter in answer. She had no more written "My Darling Will," than a knock came at the door.

"Come in," called Mattie.

Her mother entered, her eyes full of tears, and a handkerchief clutched to her face. Mattie's heart lurched, she knew something was wrong. Before she could ask, Moira spoke.

"It's over, Matilda," Moira sat on the bed, her tears spilling down her cheeks, opening her arms to hold her daughter.

"The war is over in Virginia."

The weight of the words dealt a blow. The tears were of relief in one way, but loss in another, the lost hopes of a young nation, combined with relief from four long years of perseverance. Mattie fell into her mother's arms.

"Oh, Mother! Now they can all come home."

CHAPTER TWENTY-SEVEN

Sergeant Andrew MacDonald walked into the yard of his farm, six months after the last visit. He had been on his way from Lynchburg for several days, first by train, then by foot. He was tired, although now he carried no rifle, nor any of the trappings of his former life as a soldier, except for his tattered uniform and well-worn slouch hat. He went around to the back and stopped at the well. All was quiet. The outbuildings looked a little worse for wear, they had not been painted or repaired for four years now. Then he saw the charred remains of the barn, and was surprised at how unaffected he was by the sight. Every barn for the last few miles, and some houses, lay in ruins. Why should his have been any exception?

He took off his weather-beaten hat and drank a dipper of water from the bucket that set on the well rim. Just as he heard voices in the kitchen, he looked to see Moira, Mattie and Jenna as they came out, each carrying something which had been hidden away during Sheridan's occupation.

"Andrew!" Moira's face brightened as she ran to throw her arms around his neck, forgetting the two jars of preserves she held, almost hitting him in the head in her haste to welcome him home.

"Careful, lass! Have I survived the Yankee army only to be knocked senseless by my own wife?" he laughed. Despite the deep sorrow at losing the war, he was thankful to be home in the comfort of his family. So many families would not have a man returning.

"Papa!" Mattie hugged him. His reddish hair was longer than usual, and he wore a scruffy beard. "Have you seen Will? Is he coming here?" Surely her father knew something of him, or if he had sent another letter. After all their letters had been delivered by the same soldier. She had not sent hers since he would probably not get it anyway.

Her father looked at her sympathetically, hating to disappoint her.

"No, darling, I haven't seen him." He did not know the intentions of the young man, and feared now that the war was over and he could return to Louisiana, he may simply dismiss the thought of Mattie's feelings. The passions of a young soldier in a wartime game of outwitting death daily could easily vanish once out of danger.

Mattie was obviously distressed by the lack of definite news. Andrew and Moira exchanged looks, then looking at Mattie, Andrew said, "I wouldn't expect too much lass," then he and Moira walked into the house together.

It was a bittersweet homecoming. Now they sat in the parlor together, Jenna having brought in tea. Andrew felt rested and after having a bath, the cleanest he had been in weeks. He knew he must talk with Jenna, and now was as good a time as any.

"Jenna, there's something I need to tell you. First I am grateful to you, more than I can say, for seeing this farm through the last four years. He set his cup on the tray as Jenna gathered the rest of the tea dishes.

"Well, Mr. Andrew, I wasn't about to leave Miss Moira and Miss Matilda as long as them Yankees was about the place," she said as she continued her work.

Andrew smiled. He felt awkward at his announcement. "This has been your home as long as it has been ours. Now, you're free to go. You have no obligation to us. I want you to know we bear you no hard feelings, and will help you anyway we can. It's your decision." He said it as gently as he could. She had always been like a family member, and he was genuinely concerned for her future.

Jenna looked at him as it dawned on her what he meant. The North had won, and that meant all the old ways of life would no longer be the same for the servants and their owners. She hesitated in her stacking dishes, then finishing, picked up the full tray.

"Mr. Andrew, you and Miz Moira, and Miz Mattie is like my family. I don't wants to leave you. Not jes yet anyway. We all gots to help each other right now."

Andrew admired her for her thoughtfulness and wisdom. The whole world for Blacks as well as Whites was in disorder. He knew that only by working together and toughing it out, could anyone survive. Jenna obviously knew that too.

"Thank you, Jenna, I'm truly glad. We'll pay you what we can, and we'll certainly share what we have with you."

They parted, Andrew left to ponder the next step in putting his world back together.

The next few days found him trying to adjust to a life he had abandoned for four years. Once again, he became involved in the farm. There would be spring planting to start. All the seed corn had been used during the winter for feed, and he would have to buy more. He needed to go to Newtown to see if there was any seed to be bought, and find out who could help him begin to rebuild the barn.

Mattie had been moping around the yard, seemingly at a loss as what to do with herself. Maybe it would do her good to accompany him into town. He found her sitting on the back porch steps, her chin resting in her hands.

"Why such a long face, lass? How about coming into town with me. I'll take you by the Dawson's shop." He tried to sound cheerful.

Mattie looked at him, unimpressed at the offer. "No thank you. I'd rather stay here." She knew she could never face Emmaline if she did see her, for she would want to know all about Will. Mattie couldn't stand to tell her she had not heard from him since the March letter. But her heart told her not to lose faith in Will's love.

"Very well, then. But cheer up." Her father lifted her chin with his fingertips, looking into the green eyes so much like his own.

After Andrew left, Mattie, being so restless, decided to take a walk. She went inside to change into her boots. Not really knowing where she wanted to go, she walked out the front door and stood on the porch. The Valley Turnpike was quiet. Her father had taken the wagon and Dandy, and were already out of sight in the direction of town. She wandered along the drive, picking the first spring flowers of the year, some early daffodils growing beside the dirt road. She was lost in her thoughts, walking towards the Adamses, smelling the fragrant yellow and white blossoms. She happened to look up, and saw a figure nearing her, coming from the south. That was not unusual, and she continued on her way. Probably just another returning soldier. She saw them all the time, sometimes one alone, often groups of two or three on their way home. They would usually stop and ask for water, or her mother would give them some food. Looking across the fields, she saw the first buds of the cherry trees. They would soon be in bloom, wearing the spring colors of pink against the new green of the grass. The mountains reared blue in the distance.

She looked forward, and the soldier was closer now. Who could he be? The Adamses' sons had both returned. Then she sensed something familiar about the stride, and the way he carried himself. Her heart beat faster with hope as she saw him stop, and looking at her, start to run now within a distance to recognize each other. It was Will!

He caught her in his arms, and lifted her off the ground. Mattie clung to his neck, dropping the bouquet of flowers. Holding her close, they kissed, and he buried his face in her hair.

Checking her emotions she quickly looked around to see if anyone was watching, even though she didn't care. He had come back! That was all that mattered. She stroked his face with her hand, lovingly staring into his blue eyes. Then she kissed him back.

"Oh, Will, I was afraid you weren't coming. I thought you'd gone home to New Orleans."

His jacket was tattered, and most of the red braid was worn off. He picked up the flowers that she had dropped, and handed them to her. He held her hand, squeezing it tight and looking at her face as they began to walk. He was thinner than before, and looked pale like he had when he was first brought to the farm wounded.

"I would never do that Mattie. I would have written again, but with everything that's happened, I thought I could get here faster than any letter."

He smiled as he looked at her face. She had grown prettier than last fall, more than he remembered, just as his love for her had grown. The love in her eyes was undeniable.

"I am on my way home, but I thought if it would be alright, I'd stay a few days. Maybe I can help your father with some of the farm work to pay for my stay."

Will had other motives for his visit, but he must talk to Mr. MacDonald before he could tell Mattie of his plans.

"I missed you so much Mattie. I used to lie awake and remember our reading *Ivanhoe*. You don't know how many times those memories got me through when I was cold and hungry."

"I missed you too, and I was so worried about you. Every time I heard the guns I prayed that you would be safe. Were you wounded any more?"

He shook his head, and they walked slowly toward the farm, hand in hand. Her knight had returned.

CHAPTER TWENTY-EIGHT

Will remained at the MacDonald's farm for a week, resting and preparing for the long journey home. Andrew was thankful for the help, and together they plowed the fields with a borrowed team Andrew had been lent by the Millers. He was also thankful for Will's loyalty to Mattie. They began preparations for rebuilding the barn. Will worked hard, each day finding the two men up at dawn, and not returning until nightfall. Jenna cooked their noonday meal and Mattie brought it to them wherever they were working, sitting with them as they ate, and taking the dishes back home. She was happier than she ever remembered, wishing these idyllic days would never end.

A few days before he left, as he and Andrew rested from their work of planting the spring wheat, Will decided it was time to do what he had returned to do. They sat with their backs against a large oak on the edge of the field. The sun was warm but not hot, just the kind of weather that gives one spring fever, and their afternoon rest break was growing longer than usual.

"Mr. MacDonald, I have to be leaving in the next day or two. I'm sorry I can't stay and help you build the barn."

"I understand, lad, don't apologize. You've been worth three men this week already. I know you must be anxious to get home, not to mention your parents wanting to see you. You don't know how much I appreciate your help."

Andrew sat with his head resting against the tree, his arms folded on his chest and his eyes closed. "I could never have gotten the planting done without you."

Will sat up and turned toward him, sitting cross legged, and taking a deep breath, continued.

"There's another reason I came back, Sir." He felt awkward. Asking a father for a daughter's hand in marriage was something at which he had no previous experience.

"What's that, son?" said Andrew, seeming to be dozing.

Will's heart raced. "I want to marry Matilda, and I'm asking for your consent."

The silence seemed to drag on, seconds into minutes. Will twisted a blade of grass in his fingers, as a mockingbird lit on a branch above them and began an annoying song. It seemed to be chiding him, and he was relieved when it flew away. Was Mr. MacDonald asleep? This had taken more courage than going into battle, and he dreaded having to repeat his request.

Andrew had heard. He had expected this, although the boy had said nothing until now. He also remembered his own proposal to Moira's father and knew the toll it was taking on the young man's nerves. He kept his eyes closed.

"How will you support a family? The war has wrecked the country, and I don't know what kind of job you can expect to find."

Will was caught off guard. He had expected a simple yes or no, but not a question like that.

"I . . . I haven't thought about it . . . too much, Sir. I suppose when I get home I can find some kind of work," he winced at his stammering.

"Mattie's only sixteen. Don't you think she's a little young for marriage?" Andrew needed to feel out the extent of Will's plans. How much forethought had the boy put into this? Life was going to be hard in a country fresh with the wounds of defeat. Will had not been home in two years, and Andrew had no idea how New Orleans had fared.

"I've thought of that too, Sir. She just seems more mature than most girls her age. She will be seventeen soon," he reminded her father. He was getting more uncomfortable and feeling hopeless.

Andrew decided he had tormented Will long enough, and now would offer his terms. He glanced at Will, now staring at the blade of grass he had been playing with nervously.

"I have a proposition for you, lad. I think it is best if we let you have a little time to be sure you know what you're getting into. Mattie will be seventeen in August. You will be twenty this summer, is that not right?"

Will was looking at Andrew with hope now, and nodded.

"How about if you go home, find a job, get settled in your new life," Andrew talked slowly and deliberately, "and come back when Mattie is eighteen. That way, you will both have time to decide for sure if getting married is what you want. I want Matilda to be happy. You're a good lad, and I feel sure you love my daughter. But maybe we're getting ahead of ourselves. First," he held up a hand in a gesture to emphasize, "you've got to ask Mattie if she will marry you. If she says yes, then I give my blessing after a year." He folded his arms again.

He had been very businesslike, as if he were closing a deal on livestock. Will listened intently. Then Andrew's face broke into a wide Irish grin, and he extended a friendly hand.

"Good luck, lad. I'd be proud to have you as a son-in-law."

Will accepted the handshake with obvious relief. He was so excited he wanted to shout, and with renewed energy he worked with the strength of two men that afternoon.

Mattie, too, had her thoughts on the future. She was changing from a child to a young woman, and the war had accelerated that change. There were no more innocent fairy tale days for girls her age. Most had seen death, suffering, and hardship. They could not go backwards from that. She knew Will would be leaving any day. Maybe if she wrote him and kept their love alive, he would want to marry her eventually. She schemed continuously to find a way to make the transition from a love forged in war to a lifetime together. Something in her heart told her this was right, and she could not envision life without William Hamilton.

That night, Will and Mattie sat in the parlor alone. She worked on the finishing touches of mending his clothes to start home with. They sat on the sofa together, Will had waited for this moment all day. How many times had he rehearsed his proposal in his head? Now, he turned to Mattie and took her sewing out of her lap, laying it aside, and holding her right hand. It was unexpected, and Mattie was puzzled. She thought he was being playful.

"Hey, what are you doing," she giggled. "You'll lose my needle, and they're not so easy to come by . . ." Her words trailed off as she watched him get down on one knee in front of her.

He looked steadily at her, the gentle blue eyes unchanged by all they had seen, the rakish smile she adored.

"Matilda MacDonald, I would like to ask you to become my wife." He kissed her hand and waited.

Mattie was struck dumb. Although she had wanted this, now that the moment had arrived she was at a loss to respond. Will waited patiently, a questioning look on his face.

"Gracious, Will," she stammered, and nodded. "Yes, Yes!" She felt giddy, unable to express anymore. They beamed at each other, and Will rose to his feet. Pulling her up by her hands, he embraced her and kissed her. She felt joy such as she had never known.

"I've already spoken to your father. He said we will have to wait a year." They stood gazing longingly into each other's eyes. "I want to leave tomorrow and get home as soon as I can, to find a job." He talked fast, excited at laying the plans for their life together. Mattie didn't want him to go, but with a wedding to plan for, she hoped the time would fly by.

"A year's not so long. We can write, and I'll tell you all about New Orleans. You'll like it there Mattie, I promise," he was animated as she had never seen him before.

"Well, I suppose I should spend more time learning my French, now that I have a reason to use it," she laughed.

They stayed up late, too full of hope and the promise of happiness to sleep. The next day, Will put on the threadbare Zouave jacket, took the extra clothes they provided and the food they packed for him, and set out on the 800-mile journey home.

He would walk most of the way; the train tracks having been destroyed. Mattie walked with him the first two miles, before parting.

All across the South, men were making their way slowly home by whatever means they could. Many returned to burned homes, destroyed farms, and scattered family. William Hamilton came home full of dreams for the future.

CHAPTER TWENTY-NINE

June 6, 1866

Mattie stood in front of the tall mirror, adjusting her broad-brimmed hat, her golden curls falling to her shoulders. She turned sideways and inspected the back of the white dress as best she could.

Her mother came in, dressed in black, the vivid difference in their clothing making a peculiar reflection in the mirror.

"Hurry, Matilda, we have to be at the cemetery in two hours!" She shoved a flower basket at her daughter.

"I'm ready, Mother," said Mattie, and grabbing the basket, they hurried to where Andrew waited in the buggy.

They were on their way to Winchester. Today was the dedication of Stonewall Cemetery. The people of Winchester had wanted to do something for the scattered graves of the brave dead who had fought for this Valley for four years, and paid with their lives. From all over the surrounding counties, shallow graves were removed of their remains, and now 3,000 graves marked the site of their final resting places, divided into sections for each state in the South. The ceremony would include various dignitaries, many ex-Confederate soldiers and some generals, and a procession of young maidens carrying baskets of flowers. Mattie was to walk in this procession.

The participants formed up and walked through the rows of headstones to stand around an arbor draped with bunting, in front of a mound of unknown dead. Three hundred veterans, stripped of their soldierly markings, were solemn and showed a steadfast dignity in the face of defeat. They were proud of the stand they had taken, and now stood not in battle lines but in tribute to their fallen brothers beneath the earth around them.

Any vestiges of their beloved flag or Confederate citizenship were forbidden by the victors, and they wore only plain gray. Mattie's heart was heavy with sadness, as was everyone's there that day. All she could think of were the thousands of beautiful young men like Will, the flower of a young nation, who now lay here.

The crowd was huge, over 10,000 people, and the carriages lined all the streets around the cemetery. After the ceremony, Mattie milled around with the crowd, reading the rows of names and chatting with family, friends and neighbors. Emmaline was there; they had walked in the flower procession together. As they stood in the lane between the Confederate section and the church cemetery, Mattie looked across the rows to the back of the newly dedicated ground.

A young man stood, all alone, his hat in his hands which were folded in front of him. Most of the crowd were leaving. Emmaline was talking to her, but Mattie shifted her attention, ignoring her friend, and walked toward the lone figure.

He was unaware of her approach, as he kneeled in front of a headstone and traced the letters with his fingers. Mattie read the inscription:

D. Monaghan

8th La. Vol. Inf.

Several small rows of graves marked the Louisiana section, at the back. She was behind Will, and as he became aware of someone he looked up, then rose.

"Mattie," he was obviously pleased to see her.

She didn't recognize him at first. In the year of their engagement they had not seen each other. Now twenty-one, Will had grown to manhood, and in his civilian clothes looked quite a proper gentleman. He also wore a trim black mustache, making his blue eyes contrast handsomely and reminding her of that day she had seen Capt. Dolly Richards. The resemblance still haunted her.

"Will, you didn't tell me you were coming."

Their initial awkwardness lasted only a moment, and he took her hands in his, kissing them. Her girlish figure had changed into that of a young woman, and his heart fluttered at seeing her.

"I wasn't sure myself. I just came over to find Dee," he looked back down at the headstone. Jean and Pierre had buried their friend with a note identifying him, so when his grave was found it could be marked. Will was thankful his companion had not suffered the fate he had been so afraid of for himself. Mattie watched him blink back the tears the memory called forth.

"Come on, then, let's find mother and papa," she tugged his hand as he hesitated, taking one last look back at the grave, and they walked with their heads together in conversation.

"I was hoping we could get married now, while I'm here. I know we had said August, but I've gottten a good job in my father's shipping office. I've had it for

six months, and managed to save quite a lot of money. We can stay with my parents at first, until we find a house. I thought you might like to be a part of that choice."

Mattie was elated to talk about their life together, never to be separated for long months again.

"Oh, Will, I want to. Won't it be fun, looking for our own home?"

She was so happy, it didn't seem right to feel that way in this place of sorrow, and she felt a twinge of guilt. Here she walked with her sweetheart—alive, healthy and handsome. How many girls had lost theirs, perhaps buried right here? It felt so good to be alive, she wanted to savor it, to embrace every moment.

"I'm so happy Will, I want to make you happy too."

"You do, Mattie, you always do," and he leaned down, kissing her as they stood in the lane between the rows of graves.

EPILOGUE

Will and Mattie were married that month, and returned to New Orleans where they would live as man and wife. The first years of Reconstruction were hard and ex-soldiers were treated like second-class citizens. The women of the South helped bind these spiritual wounds after the war, just as they had bandaged the physical ones during it.

One day Captain DeCourcey called, and Mattie was able to return the little flag. He had been imprisoned at Fort Delaware after being captured at Winchester, and the conditions he had been subjected to had ruined his health. He was so moved at the appearance of the little flag, he kissed Mattie on the cheek, knowing if he had not given it to her, it would have been lost.

His daughters were with him, both like Mattie now married to former soldiers, and she was impressed at how beautiful they were. She practiced her conversational French during their visit, while Will and the Captain compared war stories and fought it all over again. Will was a kind and loving husband, and she couldn't be happier.

She missed the Valley, with its mountains, and the distinctive seasons of snow and frost, spring with its redbud and cherry trees, and summer with its hazy heat. New Orleans was very different but she grew to love it too.

She would return once each year to see her parents, and they occasionally came to visit her and Will. But mostly she missed those Shenandoah autumns on the farm, with the wildly red and orange leaves of the maples, the harvesting of the apples and threshing of wheat. All the years of her life, the autumn of 1864 would forever be at the forefront of her memory.

AUTHOR'S NOTE

When I lived in the Shenandoah Valley of Virginia, it was never far from my mind what the conflict of the American Civil War was like for that region and its people. Everyday I drove to work through a battlefield, although it was not so apparent to the rushing traffic passing through, in too much of a hurry to notice the small stone markers of Colonel Mosby's engagements, or read the highway signs along the road.

Fortunately I read as much as I could about those Confederate days, when for four long years the residents exhibited the most courageous and stalwart behavior to support their sons and fathers, brothers and husbands who wore the gray.

One of the most memorable was a diary kept by a doctor's wife in Stephens City. It was called Newtown then. She had a sister in St. Albans, West Virginia and they corresponded all during the war. Most of the events in *Shenandoah Autumn* were based on true events in the life of Molly Hansford Walls.

She tells of three young men, soldiers from other Southern states, who came back after the war to marry the daughters of the families who had nursed their wounds. They are represented by the characters of Will Hamilton and Matilda MacDonald in the story. It was a time of intense living, danger, excitement and sorrow. But it was also a time which those who lived through it would never forget, and I wanted to capture all of that in the story. I hope it will inspire young readers to seek out the many diaries left by those women manning the home front and the soldiers they loved, for none can tell the story as well as those who lived it. I also wrote it for all the young Southerners who need to be aware of our proud heritage, and the truth of our history. As a daughter of the South I am aware of the lack of subject matter in general for young readers.

Newtown, Virginia where Matilda lived with her family was founded about 1758 by Lewis Stephens, and first called Stephensburg. The primary settlers in this part of the Shenandoah Valley were Scotch-Irish, but also included many Dutch, Welsh and German families. They built log houses of two stories, which were later covered in clapboards and painted white. Many of them are still standing today. Wagon-making was the chief industry.

The farms primarily raised grain crops of corn, wheat, barley and oats, as opposed to the cotton, tobacco and sugar cash crops of the Deep South. That is why it was called "The Breadbasket of the Confederacy" and was vital to the Southern war effort. Valley farms tended to be smaller and though some landowners were slaveholders, they owned mostly house servants and farm hands, like Jenna and Tom.

War came to the Valley early because of its strategic importance. Winchester, the gateway to the Shenandoah, changed hands seventy-two times.

Opposing forces would clash somewhere in skirmishes around Newtown almost daily. But there were at least eight important battles fought within twelve miles of the village. These were First, Second and Third Winchester, First and Second Kernstown, Fisher's Hill, Front Royal, and Cedar Creek. Over 30,000 men became casualties in these engagements, and many hospitals sprang up as a consequence. But for those left in the vicinity of Newtown, private homes often became the source of comfort and healing for the soldiers of both sides.

Because of the almost continual presence of both armies in the area, recovering Confederate soldiers were in constant fear of becoming prisoners if their presence was discovered by patroling Union soldiers or stragglers. Families who treated the soldiers could suffer punishments for aiding and abetting the enemy. Part of Newtown was burned by Union General David Hunter in the spring of 1864, along with outlying farms and barns. There was constant harassment by Union forces if they suspected that a family had aided any of Colonel John S. Mosby's Rangers, as a bitter rivalry existed between these partisans and the cavalry of General George Custer.

Often wounded Confederates who recovered were smuggled back to Confederate lines by women who had nursed them. Colonel Mosby was himself wounded, and brought through Union lines to safety by a black servant boy with a calf-drawn cart. Other ingenious plans involved covering soldiers with grain sacks and convincing patrols that the driver of the vehicle was "going to the mill." Because of the intimacy and bond formed through these dangerous times, many young men returned after the war to marry their young nurses and remain family members of those who had saved their lives.

I would like to thank all those who helped me get this book together. My friend Nancy Stephens and her

generous use of a computer and her house while I re-
wrote and typed. My family's patience, especially my
four-year-old son, Alex, who patiently occupied himself while Mommy sat at the kitchen table for hours
each day. Also, fellow living historian friend, Julie
Young, and her daughters, Emily and Megan, who were
the first to read the manuscript and encouraged me
tremendously.